1119

D0014846

The Prince Problem

The Prince Problem

VIVIAN VANDE VELDE

Scholastic Press / New York

To Jenn Laughran, a princess
among agents

table of contents

❧ Beginning ❧

"Once upon a time . . ."

Prince Telmund of Rosenmark loved stories of all kinds, but he had a special fondness for stories that began, so full of promise, with those words.

When a story began "Once upon a time," a prince who was the youngest—as Telmund was—could end up having wonderful adventures against fire-breathing dragons, spell-casting witches, even hungry ogres. No catastrophe was too great: Eventually everyone would appreciate him. Strangers would cheer for him in the streets. His parents would realize they had underestimated him. Those older brothers, whom everyone had been counting on, would acknowledge him. (Most stories included two thoroughly disagreeable older brothers, but in Telmund's case, there were three adult brothers, which made them more disinterested than disagreeable. But surely the same rules would apply.) And a distant kingdom's beautiful princess would swoon for love of him—either a princess who needed rescuing from something or one whose father had set a seemingly impossible test to win her hand.

No matter if that youngest prince was a bit puny, even for his age, or that he appeared to have no special talent, or that no one took him seriously. In any story that began "Once upon a time," if there was a youngest prince, you could count on knowing that he would save the day.

Telmund was waiting for his story. His once-upon-a-time. His and-then-everyone-acclaimed-the-youngest-prince tale. It was only a matter of time.

And then his mother gave birth to a fifth son.

Suddenly Telmund was not the youngest prince. Nor was he the oldest, who would inherit the kingdom and one day become king. He was just one of the middle sons—perhaps the least special of all his brothers.

Suddenly "Once upon a time" felt impossibly far away.

"Once upon a time . . ."

Princess Amelia of Pastonia hated stories that began with "Once upon a time." She preferred facts to stories, and in any case thought that *particular* sort was the most useless, especially for the only child of a royal couple. Someday—many, many years in the future, she hoped—she would reign over the lands now ruled by her parents. She needed to be ready, to be able to speak and read and write in as many languages as she could possibly learn, so that she could communicate with people of different lands. She needed to be able to do sums as easily as breathing, and to understand history, science, finances, agriculture, and diplomacy. And even—should things ever come to that—warcraft. There was no time for foolishness, or for frittering away her hours caught up in the made-up experiences of made-up people.

She loved her parents, she truly did, but she simply could not understand their fondness for make-believe. "Relax, Amelia," her father would say. "Haven't you ever heard the story about the man who was always so busy that—"

"I'm in a rush right now, Father," Amelia would cut him off, even if she wasn't in any special hurry. She simply wished to avoid having to listen to one of his stories.

"You fret too much," her mother would tell her. "Things always end up 'And then they lived happily ever after.'"

"Not without a lot of work, Mother," Amelia would point out, even though her parents *did* seem to be living a charmed, worry-free life—sort of like the end of a once-upon-a-time story but without having had to go through the middle part with the rampaging giant or the man-eating sea monster or the unwise bargain with a wicked sorcerer.

"Your father has everything under control," her mother would assure her.

Which Amelia should have taken as a warning.

❧ *Chapter 1* ❧

Surprise!

TELMUND
❧⟶❧

Telmund was supposed to be watching over his younger brother, Wilmar. This was never a task assigned to any of his older, more important brothers. Normally, Telmund didn't mind. But today was Saint Abelard Festival Day, with close-set stalls assembled on the green between the castle and the town—and all Wilmar wanted to do was whatever Telmund told him *not* to do. This included climbing onto things, leaping off things, hiding beneath things, jumping out at people from behind things, and barging through things, unmindful of the clattering of falling-down things behind him.

"Stop!" Telmund ordered, having managed to catch hold of the squirmy six-year-old. "Behave like the son of the king." As soon as he said it, he couldn't believe those words had actually come out of his mouth. People had been telling *him* to behave like the son of the king his whole life. In fact, they still said it to him, even though he was thirteen. Of course when they said it to Telmund, nobody meant *Stop running in a crowd* or *Watch*

4

where you're going or *Careful!* When they said it to Telmund, they meant *Get your nose out of that book* or *There's more to life than stories and poetry* or *Stop daydreaming.*

Telmund decided the way *not* to sound like one of his parents was to *explain* to his brother *why* his actions were inappropriate.

However, explaining would be difficult, since Wilmar was wriggling so much he was likely to leave his shirt in Telmund's hand. Running through the festival half-naked was something else the son of the king should not do.

"Listen to me!" Telmund demanded. "You knocked that man's vegetables onto the ground. He'll have trouble selling them if they're all bruised and pitted with pebbles."

The vegetable man must have recognized the two princes, for he was picking up the fallen produce without a word of complaint.

"Well, then," Wilmar said, twisting against Telmund's grip, "he can go down to the kitchen to get new ones."

"No, he cannot," Telmund said. "He is not a member of the king's family nor a castle servant. He has to grow the vegetables himself, and harvest them, and carry them to town in his cart, and sell them in order to make money to support himself and his family."

Telmund was not clear on exactly *how* one went about growing and harvesting and carting, but surely it was hard work that shouldn't be added to by the carelessness of his little brother.

Wilmar looked at the pennies in his sweaty hand, coins he had been given by the castle steward in order to buy treats. He had already been back to get more pennies twice, and his mouth

5

was still outlined with mustard, plum pudding, and powdered sugar. Even though he was more energetic than anyone had a right to be, he was not a mean-spirited child. "Will this be enough for the man to support himself and his family?" he asked, offering his handful of pennies for Telmund to see.

"No," Telmund said.

"I can get more." Wilmar resumed his wriggling so abruptly that Telmund almost lost hold of him.

"No," Telmund repeated. "It wouldn't be enough."

"How much does he need?"

"I don't know," Telmund admitted. "But more."

"Does he have more vegetables at home?"

"I don't know."

"How long does it take to grow vegetables?"

"Just tell the man you're sorry and help him pick up what you knocked over," Telmund ordered.

"You don't know much," Wilmar pointed out, but he helped the man, who was almost finished gathering up the spilled vegetables on his own. Once done, Wilmar gave him the pennies, solemnly saying, "To *help* support your family." The greengrocer doffed his hat and bobbed his head in appreciation at the gesture—though Telmund had to suspect that any common boy from town who'd knocked over the produce wouldn't have been let off so easily.

Wilmar took off at a dead run to find the steward and replace his pennies.

"Stop!" Telmund called after him.

Wilmar obeyed as well as the wind might.

Telmund took off after him, catching up more by virtue of the length of his seven-years-older legs rather than any particular speed.

Wilmar zigged just as Telmund zagged, so that all Telmund's hand closed on was the untucked hem of his brother's shirt. Both boys careened into an old woman who was just rounding the corner of a stall.

Wilmar and the old woman went sprawling onto the ground. Telmund was just barely able to keep on his feet by throwing his arms out for balance. Unfortunately, doing so knocked over the stall keeper's display of wooden bowls, which fell off the counter with a clatter.

"Clumsy oaf!" the stall keeper cried but a moment later realized to whom he was speaking. He slapped himself on the forehead and said, "What was I thinking, setting those up too close to the edge? I'm such a clumsy oaf *and* a fool!" He reached down to help the old woman to her feet, something Telmund would have done but couldn't, because Wilmar was in his way. His brother was on his hands and knees, gathering up the spilled bowls, some of which had rolled away from the stall.

"Give the man some money," Wilmar ordered Telmund, "so he can support his family."

Telmund sighed and shook his head. *He* hadn't gotten any pennies from the steward. Besides, unlike the vegetables, the bowls were only dusty, not damaged.

"How about the old woman?" Wilmar asked. "Does she have a family to support? Will you give *her* money?"

7

"No," Telmund said, his patience close to an end. Best to get Wilmar out of the festival crowds and insist that the steward take over watching him. To the stall keeper and the old woman, he added, "We're so sorry," and he grabbed hold of his brother by the ear so he couldn't get away.

"Ow!" Wilmar yelped, even though Telmund wasn't holding that hard. "You're hurting me."

"No, I'm not," Telmund said. "Tell . . . everybody . . ." He'd just realized his brother had called the old woman an old woman. She *was* old. No doubt she knew she was old. But it still wasn't good manners. "Tell them you're sorry."

But Wilmar only kept repeating, "Ow! Ow! Ow!"

Even though Telmund was barely holding on.

The old woman narrowed her eyes at Telmund. "It seems to me *you* should be the one saying you're sorry."

The stall keeper was trying to get her attention, but maybe she assumed he was just normally given to winks and jerks and throat clearings.

She continued scolding Telmund. "*You* were the one chasing *him*. Big bully that you are, and twice his age. No wonder the poor, frightened child was fleeing, so that he accidentally ran into me."

"Poor, frightened child," Wilmar echoed solemnly, doing his best to sound and look pitiful. True, he was not mean-spirited, but he *was* willing to accept coddling and spoiling from wherever it came.

Telmund shook his head, but before he could protest that the woman thoroughly misunderstood the situation, she finished,

"And then, when you thought no one was looking, you knocked over this man's goods."

"No," Telmund said, "that's not what happened at all."

"I *saw* you," the old woman insisted, demonstrating with her arm in the air how he had swept the bowls off the counter.

"But I didn't mean—"

She was about to call him a liar—he could see it on her face.

Apparently the stall keeper could see it, too. "Your Highness," he said to Telmund, obviously trying to let the old woman know that she was dealing with royalty, not common town children. It wasn't that the royal family of Rosenmark had a reputation for cruelty, but Telmund had found the townspeople treated all of them a bit anxiously in any case. Some kingdoms, after all, were afflicted with the occasional Bloody Duke or Mad Duchess.

"Thank you so much for helping me," the merchant told him. Then, just in case the woman didn't catch his warning, the merchant retreated to the farthest corner of his stall and immersed himself in sorting his bowls by size and type of wood.

"Oh," the old woman said, but not in an impressed tone of voice. In fact, it sounded to Telmund like the exact opposite of an impressed voice. "You're the king's son, are you? That makes you a royal bully. That's the worst kind."

It was time to put an end to this, by showing her that he was really very well mannered. He would start by introducing himself, move to an expression of regret for inconvenience caused, then take his leave.

"Madam, I am Prince Telmund," Telmund said, inclining his head respectfully because of her age. This gesture wasn't strictly necessary, as her clothing—ragged and stained as it was—identified the woman as a simple peasant. Still, when it came to manners, too much was better than too little. "And this is Prince Wilmar. We truly apologize for any difficulty we caused you."

"Oh," the old woman said, in a you're-*still*-not-impressing-me tone. "So you're this one's older brother?"

"Yes," Telmund told her, although there were times he'd gladly trade Wilmar in for a rock.

To Wilmar she said, "You poor dear."

Wilmar nodded his head piteously, then once again cried, "Ow!" for the tug on his ear that he himself had caused.

"Youngest brother, are you?" the old woman asked him.

The phrase, directly out of a once-upon-a-time story, made the hairs on Telmund's arms stand up, despite the warmth of the day.

"Yes," Wilmar sniveled.

Telmund let go of his brother's ear. Something about this situation felt . . . wrong. Foreboding, even. "That's enough, now," he said to Wilmar. "Let's go. Stop playing for sympathy."

It was unfair to make judgments based on appearances, but it was hard not to. With her scraggly hair and the large wart growing on the tip of her nose, the old woman really was the spitting image of . . . well, a witch.

Pair this with Wilmar, the supposedly put-upon youngest brother . . .

The old woman's gaze snapped back to Telmund. "Leave him alone," she commanded, in a tone that said she was just as used to being obeyed as the king himself.

No, no, no! Telmund wanted to protest. He wasn't a cruel older brother, really he wasn't. He was just trying to keep Wilmar from single-handedly demolishing the festival.

"We're truly sorry," Telmund said, taking a step back from her. In once-upon-a-time stories, the cruel older brothers never learned their lessons, and they never apologized.

"Not yet, you're not," the old woman said. Then she raised her hands, palms facing Telmund. "But you will be."

Telmund had read enough once-upon-a-time stories to know what was coming. "Not a frog!" he pleaded, knowing that prince-to-frog was a standard enchantment in a witchy repertoire. Frogs and toads made him squeamish. Besides, even though the castle was on an island in the middle of the river, Telmund wasn't good at swimming—an even bigger disadvantage for an amphibian than for a prince. "Please don't turn me into a frog!"

The old woman paused a moment to consider. Then she said, "All right."

And *then* she let loose with a magic spell.

AMELIA

Princess Amelia excelled in many things, but dancing was not one of them. She could admit to the charm of an attractive couple—the beautiful girl in a flowing gown, the handsome young man in his dapper garb—moving together gracefully and self-confidently, as though they and the music were all that mattered in the world. But she knew that the fluid and seemingly effortless movements took skill and practice. She didn't have the patience for that.

So when her mother announced over afternoon tea, "Your father and I have planned a ball," Amelia sighed.

Her mother pretended not to notice.

But Amelia knew royal balls were social events people expected, so she resolved not to complain. She pretended not to have sighed. "How nice," she said, managing the cool but attentive tone she'd heard from other princesses her age—princesses her parents insisted she meet but with whom she had little in common. "When?" Maybe she could arrange to be busy.

Her mother was just as cool. "Tonight," she said.

"*What?*" Amelia squeaked. Her mother's ladies-in-waiting were all sitting clustered around the window at the far end of the room to get the best light for their stitchery. They were obviously too refined to listen in, but still jumped at Amelia's unprincess-like squeal.

It wasn't that a ball was important to her, but—frivolous as they were—she knew such occasions took a lot of planning. How would any of the other princesses be able to get here in that short a time? And even if those from the nearest realms could travel quickly enough to arrive before dusk, they certainly wouldn't have time to prepare. Amelia had seen princesses preparing for balls: It took just about the whole day to select which of the five or six dresses they had brought with them to wear—usually depending on what the other princesses were wearing. Not to mention the jewels, and the shoes, and the hair arrangements . . . (Amelia had always suspected that princes didn't take quite as long to ready themselves as princesses, but she couldn't be sure.)

Oh, and what about the decorations for the castle? And then there was the writing out of invitations, and the cooking of food, and the gathering of flowers, and the moving of furniture, and the hiring of musicians . . .

"What?" Amelia repeated. "Who can come on such short notice?"

"Well," her mother said, the amusement coming through in her voice, "you."

"I don't understand."

"Your father and I have been planning this for weeks."

"Oh," Amelia said, the truth finally sinking in. She had been about to protest that a ball couldn't be put on in one afternoon. It would have to be canceled, or at least postponed. Which, of course, was exactly what her parents had known she'd do. "Why didn't you tell me?" she asked.

"I'm telling you now," her mother answered. "I know you, and I know that this gives you *plenty* of time to get . . ." Now it was her mother's turn to sigh. ". . . as ready as you'll ever get." She forced a bright smile. "We didn't want you to fret."

Or to have time to think up excuses, Amelia guessed.

"We put the visiting princesses in the east wing . . ."

"How nice," Amelia said. She had been outside with the botanist studying medicinal plants all morning and hadn't noticed.

"... and the visiting princes in the west wing ..."

"Of course."

"... and the various parents in the north wing."

"It sounds as though you've planned everything."

"Not everything," her mother said. "*You'll* get to choose which prince is to your liking."

Amelia thought about this. "You mean for the first dance?"

"No, dear," her mother answered cheerfully. "I mean to become betrothed to."

Chapter 2

Oops!

TELMUND

Telmund felt the way he imagined a dandelion gone to seed would feel if a rainbow-shimmer breeze blew it apart. And then reassembled it. Backward.

Suddenly the grass was so long it tickled his belly.

No, that wasn't right . . .

The grass tickled because his belly was so close to the ground.

Which meant he was on hands and knees.

Except he wasn't.

He was on all fours, but all fours meant four legs—four furry, gray legs. Four was twice as many as he should have, and furry was definitely alarming. When he looked down to see them, he could also see that he had long, white whiskers that evidently sprouted on either side of his nose. Snout? Muzzle?

"What am I?" he asked.

It came out: *Squeak?*

The old woman—the old witch—leaned down and said with a certain amount of smug glee, "You're a rat."

A rat? The only good thing Telmund could think about *that* was it probably meant that—unlike for a toad or frog—swimming would not be required. But still: a rat?

Wilmar, sounding more amazed than distressed, said, "Wow." He squatted for a closer look. His head was enormous, and Telmund flattened himself onto the ground, thinking, *Don't notice me*, which was a ridiculous thing to think since Wilmar clearly already *had* noticed him, and—besides—why shouldn't he? Surely, Telmund had nothing to fear from his brother. Wilmar repeated, "Wow." He turned to the witch. "Can I pick him up?"

"No," Telmund said frantically. This, too, came out: *Squeak*.

"Certainly," the witch said. "Use his tail."

"No," Telmund said again. And he repeated it, louder and faster as his brother grasped him by the tail and dangled him at eye level: "No! No! No! No!" *Squeak! Squeak! Squeak! Squeak!*

Ouch! That hurt! And the world swayed dizzyingly. Telmund suspected that rats couldn't vomit, because if they could have, he would have.

"What's he saying?" Wilmar asked, peering at Telmund closely.

"He's saying 'Squeak,'" the witch said. But then she relented. "He's saying 'No.'"

Can she speak rat, Telmund wondered, *or is she guessing?*

She added, "Don't hold him so close to your face. He may bite your nose."

Wilmar jerked his hand away, causing Telmund's world to once again careen about wildly. But then Wilmar said, "No, he wouldn't do that," and brought his hand in close once more, so

16

that Telmund's world narrowed to his brother's eyes and nose. "Is he saying *no* because he doesn't want to be a rat or because he doesn't want to be held by the tail?"

Both, Telmund thought. Why could he understand but not make himself understood?

The witch shrugged. "Hard to say," she admitted.

"He probably doesn't like either thing," Wilmar said. He placed his left arm across his chest and set Telmund down in the angle his elbow made.

It was very good to have the world stop tilting and spinning.

"Thank you," Telmund said. Since he knew it would come out as *Squeak*, he made sure he said it very calmly, so that it would sound different from his previous panicked squeaks. He fully intended to bow his head to show his appreciation for his brother's gentleness, but apparently rats don't do that, and instead he found himself brushing his paws against his whiskers.

"Hmph," the witch said. She leaned in to tell Telmund, "I don't trust you."

Which seemed positively unfair, considering who had changed whom into a rodent.

"He's cute," Wilmar said, using a finger to pet the top of Telmund's head.

It's humiliating to be called cute by your little brother.

But the head petting felt so nice, Telmund's racing heart slowed down, and he closed his eyes in enjoyment of it. Surely the witch would turn him back to his own form once Wilmar explained that Telmund was not a wicked older brother. *Tell her,* he wished at Wilmar. *But keep petting my head while you do.*

17

"Can he understand me?" Wilmar asked.

The witch didn't answer.

Telmund felt Wilmar's arm tense.

He was aware of Wilmar's torso moving as he swung his head left and right as though . . .

Telmund's eyes flew open. He squirmed around so that he was facing outward, searching left and right.

His rat eyesight wasn't as good as his Prince Telmund eyesight, but he could tell there was no sign of the witch in the festival crowd.

How could Wilmar explain to her if she wandered off?

Wilmar placed his free hand over Telmund, to keep him secure in the crook of his arm as he stood. "Did you see where she went?" he asked the stall keeper.

The man stood amongst his bowls with his mouth hanging open.

This expression clearly indicated he'd seen the witch cast her spell, but it was less clear whether he'd seen where she'd gone afterward.

"Hold on, Telmund," Wilmar said. "Cute as you are, you can't stay a rat." It was reassuring to hear him say that. Even more reassuring to hear him say, "I'll get help." He started running, with Telmund still tucked between his elbow and chest, his right hand cupped over Telmund to keep him from bouncing loose.

It also kept Telmund from being able to see where they were going. He was aware of his brother jostling through the crowd, zigging and zagging, bumping against people, people bumping against him. All this up-down-and-around was making it hard to concentrate.

Was Wilmar searching for the witch? That's what Telmund hoped he was doing. After all: Who could help him besides the witch?

Well, Telmund thought, maybe another witch. Not that he was aware of another witch living in the kingdom. On the other hand, he hadn't been aware of *any* witches—including the one who'd just bespelled him into rat-hood. Still, maybe there were other witches, friendlier witches, who could counteract her spell.

Wilmar came to an abrupt stop. In fact, he not only stopped moving forward but he was actually jerked backward. The abrupt ending of his forward momentum caused his right hand to swing away from protecting Telmund's head, and Telmund catapulted out of his brother's arm and onto the grass.

Telmund flipped, somersaulting heels over head (assuming rats have heels) for what felt like at least four or five times before skidding to a stop. He lay there on his back, looking skyward.

"What ho, Prince Wilmar?" a big voice boomed. "Where are you going in such a rush? And where's your brother who's supposed to be minding you?"

Telmund righted himself and found himself looking up, up, up to the castle steward, who—under normal circumstances—wasn't that tall a man. Especially given that he was sitting. An awning had been erected for him so he could sit in the shade, lounging on the bank of the river that encircled the castle. It was a place from which to watch the goings-on of the festival and to supervise whatever needed supervising.

"He's right here!" Wilmar cried. Then as the steward got to his feet—his big, enormous feet—he added, "Don't step on him!"

The steward focused on the first thing Wilmar had said and ignored the second. He looked in the direction from which he'd seen Wilmar running and said, "I don't see Prince Telmund. Have you been playing hide-and-seek with him while he was trying to watch you? That's a naughty thing to have done, but I won't tell your parents if you don't."

"No," said Wilmar. He scooped Telmund up and held him out on his palm for the steward to see. "He's here."

The steward's gaze swept over the two of them.

Telmund stood erect, which he estimated made him look more regal, or at least more human.

The steward made a disgusted sound. "Prince Wilmar! Put that creature down. It's vile and spreads disease."

"No, it doesn't," Wilmar said. "And it's not an *it*. This is Telmund. A witch put a spell on him."

The steward snorted. "That sounds like one of your brother's fanciful stories," he said. As though stories were a bad thing.

And with that, he grabbed hold of Telmund by the tail and flicked him away.

Through the air Telmund flew, somersaulting once more.

One somersault . . .

. . . two . . .

. . . the first half of a third . . .

. . . and into the river.

AMELIA

It took three tries before Amelia got her voice to work. "Betrothed?" she gasped. "Mother, I'm fourteen!"

"Yes," her mother said, sounding amused rather than irritated. "I remember. I was there when you were born."

"I'm too young to be betrothed," Amelia protested. But even as she said it, she knew this wasn't, strictly speaking, correct. In the world of the aristocracy, two kings sometimes forged an alliance by agreeing that one's son would marry the other's daughter. It was not unheard of for this to be decided when one or both of the children were still infants.

Sure enough, her mother smiled indulgently as she pointed out, "You're too young to get *married*, of course. But it's time to start thinking about whom you will marry. You're the one who brought up the subject."

"What?" Amelia asked. "No, I didn't. When? I never said . . . *What?*"

"Well, yes, not exactly," her mother agreed. Her mother always agreed—even when disagreeing. "But you're the one who mentioned Prince Sheridan of Bittenhelm at the Council meeting two months ago. How dangerous it is to have such an ambitious man on our border, just waiting for his father to die so *he* can rule as he chooses."

"But his father survived the fever he had," Amelia protested. Still, even as she said it, she knew he might not survive his next. King Whitcomb was old—old enough that he had reigned

21

longer than her *own* father had been alive—and it was only the friendship he bore her father that had kept the kingdom of Pastonia safe.

A feeling of horror washed over Amelia. "You haven't invited Prince Sheridan to this ball, have you? You aren't thinking—"

"No," her mother hastened to say. She was too refined to look horrified, but she couldn't avoid the look of distaste. "Not an alliance *with* him, one to protect you *from* him."

Well, that was a relief, seeing as Sheridan was closer to her parents' age than her own. Amelia knew little of the man, but his public actions so far had proven him self-serving and quick-tempered. During his father's latest illness, he had recommended that—*should* his father survive—it would probably still be best for the country of Bittenhelm if the elderly king stepped down from power, in order to let someone more fit rule.

Amelia wanted to protest that she didn't need protecting, but she knew that wasn't the way of the world. Besides, she suspected this would only serve to make her parents firmer in their resolve.

Her mother smiled and nodded. "And of course you will have your choice." But her mother knew Amelia well enough to add, "Though you cannot choose *not* to choose."

Then her mother leaned in close to whisper, even though there was no one nearby to listen in, "It doesn't have to be at this ball. If there's no one to your liking tonight, we'll find another way." She squeezed Amelia's hand. "And nothing permanent will be decided tonight, in any case. If you do think you like one of the princes you dance with tonight, you'll have a chance to get to know him before announcements are made. Although I must remind you that your father and I had an arranged marriage, and I was only two years older than you are now. It's turned out to be perfect in every way." She kissed Amelia's cheek. "You are the proof of that."

Amelia sighed. How can you argue with your mother when she says things like that?

"Now go greet the other princesses and get ready."

Unenthusiastically, maybe even dragging a bit, Amelia made her way to the east wing. The guest chambers there opened onto a central common room, which had many windows to let in enough light to be able to distinguish nuances of color. This feature was essential, lest some unfortunate princess accidentally chose a crimson bow, thinking it scarlet to match her dress, and have to suffer humiliation once her mistake was seen.

Mirrors had been gathered from all over the castle: hand mirrors to scrutinize up close and wall mirrors to get the full effect. And of course there were assorted couches for resting on, should a princess tire herself during the exhausting work of beautification.

Amelia could hear the princesses' fluttery voices—laughing in delight, weeping in frustration, or gossiping in conspiratorial whispers—before she even got to the door. Once she stepped into the room, she was met with an almost overpowering haze of perfumes and powders, along with the sight of more lace and ruffles and glittering gems than any one room should be expected to hold. There were at least two dozen princesses in various stages of readiness. Likely there were even more in their own private rooms, overcome by the strain and needing quiet ministering from their attendants. All around Amelia, maids were being praised, scolded, or encouraged to sew beads onto bodices faster.

Her own maid, Constance, must have been waiting by the door, for she took Amelia by the elbow and led her through the throng of princesses to the area of the room where her things had been laid out. Constance had helpfully brought everything out from Amelia's chamber, so that she could choose whatever she wanted while basking in the companionship of her guests.

Amelia couldn't help but notice that some of the princesses had brought more garments with them than she possessed here in her own home.

"Hello, Princess Amelia," several of the princesses called to her. Amelia was aware of a few others quietly asking one another, "Who's that, again?" She didn't hold it against anyone for not recognizing her, though she herself made a point of memorizing names and faces. Addressing someone personally was a courteous thing to do and made people—whether guests or servants—feel welcome and appreciated.

Still, it was sometimes hard to tell one frill-bedecked and ribbon-festooned beautiful young princess from another. This was especially true of the triplets from Ostergard—Selena, Serena, and Serafina—who all had huge green eyes, blonde hair in loose ringlets, cute little upturned noses, and not a sensible thought amongst them. But Amelia was confident she made no mistakes.

"Does this gown make me look fat?" the tall and willowy Princess Colleen asked her.

Amelia could have said, *You KNOW that you couldn't look fat even if you stuffed pillows around your waist, and you're only asking because you're seeking out compliments*, but she simply said, "Not at all. You look lovely."

Princess Roselyn needed reassuring, too. "Does this sapphire and diamond necklace make me look faded out?" she asked breathlessly. She always said *everything* breathlessly. Roselyn brushed her hair back, as though there was any chance of anyone missing the necklace, which was nearly as wide as a man's belt. "There are so many diamonds, I'm worried the light shining off all those facets will reflect onto my face and make me look pale."

Amelia could have said, *Yes, we all see your necklace, which no doubt cost enough to feed a dozen villages for a year*, but she only said, "It brings out the sparkle in your eyes."

Princess Esmerelda sidled close and whisper-asked, "Is my gown prettier than Christabelle's? She's always trying to look prettier than me."

Amelia whisper-answered, "She never could."

And when Princess Christabelle pulled Amelia aside to ask her the same thing, Amelia gave *her* the same answer.

Several of the princesses had changed their minds and ordered their maids to fetch alternate gowns—which of course necessitated different shoes, different jewelry, and different hairstyles. Three of the maids, having been through this several times already, were crying softly as they worked. One bore a bright red handprint on her cheek.

"Which gown would you like?" Constance asked Amelia.

"The yellow one that's on top will do fine," Amelia said, even as she overheard someone talking about a princess who wasn't there. Someone who'd shown up at a ball the previous week wearing a yellow dress.

"And, my dear, she looked like a daffodil. I am not exaggerating one bit: a daffodil!"

Constance raised an eyebrow, to question whether this comment had made Amelia change her mind. Her hand hovered over the dress right below the yellow one, which was blue.

Amelia leaned close to whisper, "I like daffodils."

"Very good, my lady," Constance said with a straight face.

Amelia let Constance choose the jewelry that would offset the dress nicely, for she had little sense of what went with what. Then Constance worked on Amelia's hair. Amelia always had trouble getting her hair to cooperate. Sometimes, when she brushed it herself, she developed knots that she had to tuck under the unknotted strands.

But hair care was something else at which Constance was skilled. Somehow the maid also had time to weave a crown of flowers—including daffodils—which she placed on Amelia's head.

"Very nice," Amelia said. "Thank you." She was not good at selecting, but she could recognize that Constance had brought out her best features.

She turned and saw that many of the princesses had stopped primping and were looking at her.

"Oh," said Princess Angelica, "are we doing flowers?"

"Well, it *is* spring," Princess Gilda said, ripping the tiara off her own head. "Gold and gems will cheapen the evening. Maggie! Maggie! Go fetch some flowers!"

"I think I'll check on my parents," Amelia said, and slipped out of the room before the chaos could truly take hold.

At least, she thought, *no one said anything about betrothals.* It would have been humiliating to have everyone know her parents were desperate to find a match for her. And she was fairly certain that if one of the princesses *had* known, they all would have. Quite a few of them—the triplets Selena, Serena, and Serafina came to mind immediately—would have been totally incapable of not blurting out such news.

Servants bowed and smiled to Amelia as she walked the halls down to the ballroom. The ball had officially begun. She could hear the murmur of voices and stringed instruments playing soft music. The visiting parents were in there, and if not all the princes, then certainly most of them.

Oh dear, Amelia thought as she realized she was the first princess to arrive. All the rest, apparently, would be fashionably late.

Seven princes spotted her right away and headed in her direction, two of them actually jostling each other to get there first. *Do they know?* Amelia wondered. Or were they just acknowledging her as the host princess? And the only princess currently within sight?

Three princes arrived a step before the others. They bowed deeply, presenting to the slower four a close view of their buttocks.

"A dance?"

"May I have the honor?"

"Shall we?"

All three spoke at once, and each extended a hand to her.

A couple of the ones in back reached around them to offer their hands, too.

It was going to be a long night.

Chapter 3

Lost and Sad

TELMUND

The water closed over Telmund's furry little head. *I'm going to drown*, he thought, *and will never have a proper funeral.* It was a shame that he wouldn't get to hear what people would have said about him. Not that he would have overheard them in any case, but people generally said nice things about someone who'd died. Telmund would have liked to hear something about himself that didn't include the phrases "nose stuck in a book" or "head in the clouds." Even Albert the old hayward had been acclaimed once he was dead. People forgot all their former grumblings that he was too lazy to take proper care of the fences and hedges in his charge. Never mind that cattle had wandered off regularly and that no one dared complain while he was alive because of Albert's foul temper—accompanied by his dead-on aim flinging cow pats.

Once he was gone, Albert had simply done the best he could, and he became prickly but fair.

Maybe they'll call me an idealistic visionary, Telmund thought. That sounded better than *impractical daydreamer*.

Of course, his little brother, Wilmar, would eventually convince their parents of what had happened. After all, the bowl seller had seen the whole thing. He could corroborate Wilmar's account of the witch. But even if they dragged the river, how likely would they be to find the body of one small rat?

On the other hand, Telmund had heard people use the expression *looking like a drowned rat*. Surely that implied rats were bad swimmers. The river below him may well have been full of rodent corpses.

Maybe the body of another rat would be pulled out and honored at his funeral.

Except . . .

Except he hadn't drowned yet.

He had bobbed up to the surface of the water, and his little ratty paws and feet seemed to be doing a better job of keeping him afloat than his own human arms and legs would have been capable of.

As irksome as Wilmar could be (which was very), family loyalty would cause him to fuss enough (Wilmar was a champion fusser) that the castle steward would start to wonder if perhaps the rat he'd thrown into the river *had been* more than a rat. The steward might take into account that, if he was responsible for drowning one of the king's sons, then a swift and well-deserved punishment was sure to follow.

Could the steward swim? Telmund wondered if he would risk his dignity by jumping into the river, *just in case* Wilmar's frantic shouts about the rat being his brother were true. Or would he squander valuable time by looking for some lackey to send into the water?

Where *were* Wilmar and the steward?

Telmund had been paddling anxiously, intent on keeping his head above water. Now he managed a quick glance toward the bank. Wrong bank, because there was nobody there. Thinking he must have gotten twisted around, he looked toward the other bank. No one there, either.

No one.

At all.

His eyesight as a rat wasn't as keen as he was used to, but there was no Saint Abelard Festival. No castle. Just rolling fields, and beyond them forest.

With much frantic paddling, Telmund managed to turn himself around, facing the direction from which he'd come. He could just barely make out the top of the castle, its spires showing off in the distance. This was the right direction to be looking, but trees blocked the festivities on the green. He was being swept downstream. The flow of the river felt much stronger on his little rat body than it had been those times he'd tried swimming as a boy. Industriously as he paddled, he continued to be swept farther and farther away.

By the time he realized that swimming upstream was a lost cause, he had bypassed the fields and was surrounded by forest. Trees crowded the river's edge. Now he concentrated on getting to the bank—either bank. But the river was wider here. Wider still from a rat's perspective. Every time he got close, some eddy or current flung him back toward the center.

And then, up ahead, a waterfall. Not much by human standards. A boy his age probably could have stepped over it, but only a boy who *hadn't* left his human form behind on the festival grounds. If anything could have given Telmund the strength to paddle to safety, it should have been the sound of the surging, tumbling water. But no. The river dragged him closer and closer to the cascading falls—then sent him catapulting over rocks that could gash him or knock him senseless.

But they did not.

Not this time, anyway.

It seemed such a simple goal: Get to the edge and climb out of the water.

But mile after mile, hour after hour, the river carried him farther from home. Forests and cultivated fields alternated with one another. He spied three more castles—never as close to the water as his family's own island castle. Maybe one of them might be the home of his second-oldest brother, Baldwin. Telmund's sense of geography was not his strongest virtue.

In any case, there wasn't anyone around to pay heed to his little rat cries for help.

Until finally—*finally*—the river narrowed. There was a mill on the left-hand bank, with its big wheel churning up water. Surely he could get to the right-hand side before he was swept up by the wheel. He paddled for all he was worth.

Then, a miraculous stroke of luck: A boy only a couple years older than Wilmar stood on the bank and seemed to catch sight of him.

"Help!" Telmund cried. *Squeak!*

The youngster took a step forward. Yes! He *had* seen! The kind child was going to wade in and pluck Telmund from the river!

Or not.

Why was the boy leaning down? What was he picking up? A stone, Telmund realized, just as the boy drew his arm back and flung with all his might. The splash of the stone caused water to spill into Telmund's mouth as he opened it to cry for help once again.

Not content with his near hit, the boy picked up a second stone. This one landed short as well.

The third made a wooden *thud!*

Before Telmund could work out *why* a stone should sound wooden, he realized something was lifting him out of the river, higher and higher into the sky . . .

The mill wheel had caught him up.

And then it brought him down again, dunking him into the water.

Telmund stopped fighting to get to the edge of the river and concentrated all his energy on not swallowing any more water. He was long since out of the range of the stone-throwing boy, and he could *not* let his weary body give up. He knew that eventually, about a five-day journey from Rosenmark, the river would empty into the sea. How long would it take for a newly formed rat to float all that way? Surely he would find some way to make it to the shore by then. Wouldn't he?

Unless he died first.

It would be so easy to stop struggling and let the river have him. The river or . . .

There was something in the water up ahead. *Something that eats rats?* he wondered, with what was not nearly the level of alarm he should be experiencing. But after being terrified for so long, Telmund was feeling more of a numb dread than an oh-my-goodness-what-am-I-going-to-do? panic.

He squinted into the distance. As much as he *didn't* want to know what was ahead, still—even more—he *did*. But he couldn't make out what was in the water. Some beast lying in wait for whatever—whomever—the river carried downstream? Whatever it was, it was motioning him closer with long arms. And many, many beckoning fingers. *That* would send a chill up the spine of boy or rat. What ghastly nightmare could it be?

My eyes are failing, Telmund thought. Everything was growing dim. The river had carried him again into a wooded area; naturally, it was darker in the woods than out in the open, but even so, this was too dark.

Still, this evidence of the coming end didn't spur him to struggle against his oncoming fate. With an unspeakable horror lying in wait just ahead, maybe drowning would be the easier fate . . .

Until Telmund realized—not with a sudden jolt but a dawning awareness—that it wasn't a living creature waiting in the water. It was the bough of a tree that had fallen into the river. And it was the smaller branches—not fingers—that were stirring so lifelike in the current.

I must get to that branch, he thought—rather more hazily than resolutely, he knew. It was his only chance of survival.

Still, even recognizing this, he didn't have the strength left to swim.

But one of those beckoning branch-fingers was close. Close enough that Telmund managed to catch hold of it with his flailing little rat paw as he swept past. He lurched to a stop so abruptly that his feeble grip almost released. But it didn't.

Now what? he wondered.

It took him a moment to answer his own question: *Climb.*

The branch was slippery with rot, but Telmund managed to lift himself up out of the brackish water.

Then to the main bough.

Then, on legs so weary they were shaking, across to the land. Blessedly not moving, not out-to-fill-his-nose-and-mouth *land.* Now that he was out of the river, Telmund became aware of how cold the water had been. And, he realized, there was nothing wrong with his eyes. The sun had simply set. It was night.

Lots of things that would love to dine on a rat would be prowling at night, he realized. Hunting.

Nonetheless, exhausted, he curled into a little rat ball right where he was and fell asleep.

AMELIA
꧁ꙮ꧂

"So I said to the duke," Prince Hagen was telling Amelia as they danced, never noticing that her eyes were beginning to glaze over, "'you may be a duke,' I said, 'but obviously you don't know as much about hunting boar as you think you do.' I mean,"—Hagen paused, but only for the briefest moment to give a dismissive sniff; he *never* stopped talking for longer than a breath or a sniff—"it's not the same thing as hunting deer. Not the same thing at all."

"Well . . ." Amelia said. But not fast enough.

"This had to be last fall," Hagen continued, "because we were there for the wedding of the Earl of Estwallen—which was a lavish affair, really almost bordering on being overdone, don't you think? You were there, weren't you? Everyone was."

Amelia was nodding, but Hagen didn't wait for an answer before continuing.

"Oh no, wait a moment. It was in the spring, because it wasn't the wedding itself—they had just announced the wedding banns . . . a much more tasteful affair. No, no, wait—I'm wrong. It *was* the fall. I remember now, because the horse I usually favor for boar hunting had come down with colic. My father's foolish equerry would have missed the diagnosis—thought the horse needed its teeth filed. 'It's not his teeth, it's his innards,' I said to the incompetent man—so it's a good thing I know horses as well as I do. There was one time—"

"Excuse me," Amelia interrupted—very bad manners indeed, but Hagen could move from one topic to the next effortlessly and endlessly. If only he could dance half so smoothly. "I need to . . ."

It was as though Hagen's endless prattling had sucked all the words out of her. She couldn't think how to finish that thought. She could have said, *I need to let my toes recover from your stepping on them*, but that would have gone beyond bad manners to being inexcusable.

No matter. Hagen had spotted one of the triplets—Serafina— for the moment without a dance partner. "That's quite all right," he said to Amelia. "Which one is that? Serena?" But he didn't wait for her answer, heading off to intercept whichever one it was before she could get away. Most of the princesses were very good at evading Hagen, making Amelia his best option.

Amelia limped off the dance floor. Yes, admittedly she was an indifferent dancer, but even given that, some of the princes seemed more prone to step on her toes than they should have been.

Her parents, who were excellent dancers, moved across the floor like two people in love, which was exactly what they were. They had eyes only for each other and wouldn't have even noticed Amelia, except that she was in too big a hurry to get some distance between herself and Hagen—the worst of the toe crushers—in case Serafina saw him coming and managed to escape.

Fleeing may have been too strong a word for Amelia's current flurry of movement—or it may not—but in any case she crashed right into one of the servants. The poor man had been carrying a tray full of tarts and pies to set out on one of the long tables that lined the room.

Dishes clattered to the floor in an aromatic explosion of broken crockery, crumbled pastry shells, and jellied fruit. The mess splattered not only Amelia and the servant but the gowns and legs of the nearest guests.

"Oh, I'm so sorry," Amelia said, mortified.

It was her voice, rather than the sounds of culinary mis-chance, that caught her parents' attention. Oblivious to the chaos around her, they each held one arm out, inviting her to dance in a threesome with them. Which would have been fine had she been three years old.

Amelia shook her head.

"Any likely prospects?" her mother called over to her.

Amelia hoped no one could guess what she was talking about, and once again shook her head.

Luckily, her parents believed in love at first sight and other such storybook conventions, so they didn't press her to try harder.

Meanwhile, Amelia could see that Serafina had hurriedly invited the aged father of one of the princes to dance, and now Hagen was heading back in Amelia's direction. Undeterred by the servants who had swarmed around her to clean up the spilled foodstuffs, he was closing in.

Her father, noticing where she was looking, winked at her, then swirled his wife around, all in perfect time to the music, blocking Hagen so that Amelia was able to make her escape.

There were six sets of doors leading outside, and she chose the closest. A little later into the summer, there would have been couples dancing out here, but this spring evening was a bit chilly for that. Even though there was light from the many doors to the ballroom and from lanterns affixed to poles, Amelia found herself blissfully alone.

Concerned that the probably perfectly nice (for someone else) but clumsy and boring Hagen might have noted her exit, she lifted the skirt of her gown up above her ankles and hurried down one of the paths of the ornamental garden.

So much had happened since she'd been in the garden with the botanist that morning. Just hours ago, Amelia had no worries beyond learning the Latin names and medicinal properties of the local plants; now she didn't even linger to enjoy the scents. She kept moving, zigzagging through the gardens until she found herself by the river that formed the northern border of the park.

She flung herself onto one of the benches there and waited for her heart to stop thudding, listening intently for any sounds that might indicate a tiresome prince had followed her. All she could hear was the chirping of frogs and crickets. Not even the distant sound of music from the ball lingered in the air.

She rested her head on the back of the bench and looked up into the star-sprinkled sky. Slowly, Amelia gave way to feeling sorry for herself.

Maybe it was because the occasion had been a ball—and balls are meant to be bright and merry and lighthearted—but each of the princes to whom she'd spoken that night had seemed young and empty-headed.

Of course her parents had invited people her own age, so they not only *seemed* young, they *were* young.

But so was she.

Which left empty-headed.

Maybe it was expecting too much to hope that princes who were close to her age would want to discuss politics and world affairs and advances in science, but that was what interested her. She did *not* want to discuss hunting or horses or which prince could belch the loudest.

Amelia sighed.

Someone behind her—someone she hadn't realized was there—said, "Star light, star bright . . ."

Amelia jumped.

But it wasn't Hagen stepping out from the shadows, or any of the other princes or princesses from the ball. Nor was it any of the parents or servants. It was a little girl.

The girl couldn't have stood any taller than Amelia's shoulder, which would have made her about ten. Her features, however, seemed to be of an older girl.

The girl stood backed against one of the juniper bushes, looking as if she had just stepped out from its leafy depths. Or maybe she was ready to shrink directly into it, should Amelia speak crossly to her.

Perhaps in the daylight, Amelia would have been able to place the girl. She must have been the daughter of one of the castle staff. But here, in the night, so far from the candlelight and lanterns of the castle and with only the glow of moon and stars to see by, it was hard to make things out. The moonlight played tricks with colors, bleaching them, so that Amelia's own dress looked gray, and the child's hair silver.

"I'm sorry," the child said, and again her voice gave the impression of a much older girl. "I didn't mean to frighten you."

"Startled," Amelia corrected, for it was important to use precise words.

The child nodded, then asked, "Wishing on a star?"

"There's no such thing as wishes," Amelia said.

Apparently the child was a stickler for precision also, for she answered, "Anyone can *wish*. The question is: Will those wishes come true?"

Because the child sounded more mature than anyone to whom Amelia had spoken in the last several hours, she answered, "By the law of averages, some of those wishes would *have* to come true."

The girl seemed tickled by Amelia's answer, and she laughed. "But does the wishing ever *cause* the coming true?"

"No," Amelia said.

"That's a very sad answer."

Amelia didn't want to make anyone sad, so she only shrugged. Then she tipped her face up once more to the night sky. *If I believed in wishes, what would I wish for?* she asked herself.

That was easy. Normally, a princess should probably be careful about sharing secret wishes with strangers. But something about the night or about the girl made Amelia wistful. "I would wish for a solution to the vile and dangerous Prince Sheridan of Bittenhelm, who covets our land."

Too bad wishes didn't come true, at least not in the sense the little girl meant.

Amelia sighed and stood up.

And looked around.

The little girl had retreated as soundlessly as she'd come, seeming to have melted into the shadows of the park.

41

Amelia walked along the river path, for this would circle around and bring her to another door in the castle. She wouldn't have to reenter through the ballroom.

The moonlight was bright enough that it caught something silver-colored on the tree-studded grass between the path and the water. Silver, like the mysterious girl's hair. Amelia took a step closer.

Ew, it was a rat that had apparently drowned and been washed ashore.

Amelia liked animals, but that didn't include rats. She considered whether she should nudge the dead creature back into the water. But that might leave a nasty mark on her shoe, and she didn't want to make more work for Constance than she needed to.

She continued following the path back to the castle.

Chapter 4

A New Day, No Better than the First

TELMUND

Telmund awoke cold and aching all over. And something nearby smelled really, really bad. Had he been sick during the night? A fever might explain the strange dream he'd had, about a witch enchanting him into a rat.

Except the more he awoke, the more he knew it hadn't been a dream.

Telmund opened his eyes and saw the blue sky above. He'd been sleeping on the ground. Outside.

Definitely not a dream.

His shoulders and arms ached from the long—endlessly long—effort to stay afloat in the river. Stretching his hands out in front of him, he remembered how unwilling the water had been to let go of him.

His . . . hands.

Something was wrong.

No, wait. The opposite was true: Something had stopped being wrong.

43

Telmund looked at his hands. They were human hands, not little rat paws. He patted his arms with his human hands. He touched his human face. He hugged his human self. He said aloud, "I'm a boy again." It came out in his human voice, not a squeak!

Apparently, the witch had felt that one day of rat-hood was enough to teach him a lesson. Never mind that he had almost drowned—several times—during his ordeal. It was over now. All he had to do was figure out how to get home.

Well, of course he could follow the river, but it was meandering and flowed over some rough terrain. The faster, easier solution was to find someone, announce who he was, explain that his father would offer a huge reward for the return of his son— even one of his younger sons—and arrange to borrow a horse.

Telmund looked around. There was a bench just over there by the juniper bushes, and a path of crushed stone: proof that someone lived nearby. Good. He hadn't eaten since snacking on some sweets at the festival yesterday afternoon, and he was looking forward to a good meal. How far away from home was he? Would the people of this land—whatever land it was—recognize his father's name?

Don't be silly, he told himself. Of course they would. He hadn't drifted *that far* downstream.

Telmund stood up. He had been lying faceup, which meant that while his front had dried in the sun, the back of his shirt and breeches hadn't. It was an unpleasant sensation to have the cold, wet clothing clinging to his backside.

And once again, he caught that awful stagnant stench. To his horror, Telmund realized it came from himself—from his river-soaked clothing. While he'd been a rat, he hadn't noticed the smell of rotting vegetation in the river water. Well, he'd noticed, but he hadn't thought of it as bad. Now he saw that the bank where he'd crawled up last night was slick with decayed leaves from the fallen branch that had been his salvation.

His knees were muddy, as were his hands. He'd left muddy handprints on his sleeves when he'd been checking himself out. He'd touched his face, too, which meant . . .

He rubbed the back of his hand across his crusty cheek, trying to clean himself up a bit. Picked something dark green and slimy out of his hair.

Someone was coming. Telmund could hear heavy footsteps on the gravel path.

I may not look presentable, he thought, *but I can* speak *presentably.*

Two men—clearly soldiers by their dress and their weaponry—rounded the bend and saw him.

Telmund bowed. "Greetings from the Kingdom of Rosenmark," he said.

But that was all he had time to say before the men took several quick strides forward and grabbed hold of him roughly.

"Who are you?" one demanded, shaking him, while the other cuffed Telmund's ear and demanded, "What are you doing so close to the castle?" Then both men said, "You aren't permitted!"

Castle? He was close to a castle? That was good news, despite the harsh treatment that had left his ear ringing. The ruler of a kingdom only a day's journey downriver would without a doubt recognize his father's name.

"I am Prince Telmund of Rosenmark," he said. "Son of King Leopold. By mischance I—"

"Got lost during the ball last night, did you?" one of the men sneered.

"Naw," the other scoffed. "Must of been before. Forgot to put on his fancy dancing duds, this prince did."

"What?" Telmund said. It was hard to make sense of what the men were saying. That could have been a residual effect of the blow to his head, or from spending the greater part of the last day only moments away from drowning, or from sleeping on the ground, or from the spell itself. Or it could have simply been that the men were making no sense.

But he could tell he was being mocked. Enough was enough.

"Unhand me!" Telmund demanded. He jerked back.

There was a ripping sound as his sleeve came loose in the one soldier's grip.

This sudden release caused Telmund's feet to go out from under him on the slick bank. Down he went, smacking his head on the fallen tree branch.

And the sky ceased to be blue and closed in on him.

Telmund woke up, facedown in the dirt, to darkness. He wondered if he had knocked himself out for an entire day, or if he had knocked himself blind.

But no, when he raised his head, he saw there was light, just not much. Only what was coming in through the chinks of some not-very-well-constructed wooden walls.

By the tools propped up against those walls, and by the shelves with pots holding dead or dying plants, he realized he was in a gardening shed. The soldiers must have carried him here until they could figure out what to do with him. No doubt the door was locked, or at least barricaded from the outside.

Still, that wasn't Telmund's biggest problem. The biggest problem was with his body. Not that he was blind. *That* would have been simple.

It was a rabbit's body.

AMELIA

Amelia joined her parents in their sitting room to have breakfast. The most courteous thing to do, after a ball, would have been to share the meal that had been laid out for the visiting princesses in the common room of the east wing. But Amelia didn't have the patience to spend any more time with them. They would spend all morning discussing the events of the previous evening. *Did you see this, that, or the other thing?* they'd ask one another. (*Yes, of course I saw,* would be the most genuine answer. *I was there, you know.* Though a more tactful response would be, *Mmmm . . .*)

Except Amelia hadn't truly been there for all of the ball. While brushing Amelia's hair this morning, her maid, Constance, had brought her up on the most noteworthy occurrences she'd missed by leaving early:

1. Prince Hagen had sworn his undying love for and longstanding devotion to one of the triplets from Ostergard, Selena. He'd spoken so prettily that Selena had accepted Hagen's proposal of marriage and told him to formally ask her father for her hand.

2. But as the evening progressed, it became obvious that Hagen couldn't truly tell one sister from the other.

3. Miffed, all three princesses took turns pretending to be the one who was betrothed to him . . .

4. Until the end of the evening, when Hagen approached their father. All three girls gathered around then, and one by one they denied ever having spoken to him.

5. Everybody else had a good time.

Now, as Amelia sat at the table, she was just in time to hear her father say, "Perhaps we could have a contest. Good morning, Amelia."

"Good morning, Father. Good morning, Mother. What kind of contest are you talking about?"

A servant placed a napkin on her lap and poured her a glass of honeyed pomegranate juice.

"I don't know," her father admitted. "Physical prowess? The last dragon was routed from the region during my grandfather's day, and there aren't any monsters in the vicinity to overcome . . . I suppose we could have a tournament."

"Ah!" Amelia said. "You're looking for something to keep the princes occupied." She nodded to a second servant, who placed a just-buttered slice of toast on her plate. How long had her parents invited the princes and the princesses to stay?

"Well, yes," Amelia's mother said, as yet another servant whose tray held little bowls of jams leaned in to Amelia and quietly offered, "Strawberry, blueberry, marmalade."

"But also . . ." Amelia's mother continued, "you know, to help you choose."

Amelia shook her head at all the jams and motioned for the other servants with *their* trays to withdraw. "Choose," she repeated, her appetite gone. "As in . . ."

"Mmmm," her mother murmured, selecting that moment to bite into a pastry.

Amelia answered her own question. "A husband. So, I'm to choose a husband based on his ability to knock other prospective husbands off a horse."

"Or we could have a contest of wits," Amelia's father suggested.

"Did you talk to any of them?" Amelia asked.

"Don't be unkind," her father told her. "You have been blessed with a keen and inquisitive mind, but remember that people can have other qualities that are equally worthwhile."

Amelia considered. Her philosophy teacher was very good at tripping people up with words; the blacksmith—who wasn't very good with words at all—knew everything there was about making steel; her mathematics teacher knew all about numbers, but not much about people; and her nanny, whom *nobody* would have called smart about *anything*, had always known how to keep Amelia from getting bored on a cold and rainy afternoon.

"I'm not saying a prince would need to be scholarly before I'd consider him," Amelia said. "But it would be nice if he could talk about something beyond his ability to play his realm's national anthem with his armpit."

"Really?" her mother asked in a tone of polite doubtfulness.

"Prince Bavol," Amelia said, "and Prince Jesper and Prince Alwyn. They had a competition. I'm amazed you missed it."

"Indeed." Her mother dabbed at her mouth with her napkin.

Her father looked amused, which Amelia found irritating.

Fortunately, at that point, there was a knock on the door.

The castellan—the improbably skinny man who had been in charge of running the castle for as long as Amelia could remember—entered and bowed to the king. "Your Highness. Ordinarily, I would not trouble you, but given the number of royal personages visiting for the ball, I wasn't sure if this matter warranted more concern than under normal circumstances."

Amelia's father nodded for him to continue.

"The castle guards have apprehended a young man on the grounds, too scruffy to be an attendant to one of the guests, yet too well-spoken to be a common miscreant. We believe he may not be quite right in the head."

"How so?" Amelia's father asked.

The castellan hesitated. "He did claim to be a prince."

Amelia's father raised an eyebrow. "Have we misplaced one of those?"

"No, Your Highness. All are accounted for. This interloper looks to be younger than any of the young men invited, and his clothes are ragged and filthy. *He* is ragged and filthy. For an imposter, he has made no effort to appear as what he claims to be."

Her father said, "So if he's a spy, he's not a very accomplished one."

"Spy?" Amelia blurted out.

Her father shrugged, but it was too late.

"Who would want to spy on us?" she asked.

"No one," her father answered. "Apparently, this is some poor, deluded simpleton."

"But who were you considering he might be?" Amelia looked from her father to the castellan. Without warning, the castellan was finding the ceiling to be infinitely fascinating, and her father had a speck *she* certainly couldn't see that he suddenly and desperately needed to get off his cuff. Her mother was smoothing out her already perfectly arranged dressing gown.

What was it that they were worried about?

Or who?

There was only one person Amelia could think of who would cause that kind of concern. "An agent of Prince Sheridan of Bittenhelm?"

"Not likely, my lady," the castellan assured her.

But the idea didn't seem to take him by surprise.

"Did Prince Sheridan know about the ball?" she asked her parents.

"He was not invited," her father said.

"That wasn't what I asked."

"Amelia," her mother said in reproof, either for her tone or for continuing to ask questions the adults obviously didn't want to answer.

Amelia crossed her arms over her chest and waited. An awful thought was gnawing at her stomach. The ball . . . The prospect of a tournament . . . . "Has Prince Sheridan . . . ?" How did someone ask without sounding full of herself? But this wasn't just about *herself*; it was about the kingdom. "Has he expressed an interest in me?" She was looking at her mother when she asked, and her mother looked down at the eggs congealing on her plate.

"We will not allow that to happen," her father assured her.

No, they would offer her up to the most promising immediate taker instead. *Promising* as defined by skill in a tournament, or perhaps the ability to solve riddles.

"Excuse me," Amelia said, setting aside her breakfast and standing.

The seriousness of the situation was emphasized by the fact that neither of her parents told her it was rude to leave before finishing her meal.

Probably, she realized, they were eager for her to leave so that they could discuss more openly. It was unfair of her parents to treat her as a child when she felt she was more responsible and mature than either of them.

Mostly, however, she was angry with Prince Sheridan for being the kind of neighbor who *made* people worry.

She stepped out of the castle and saw one of the guards standing there, not exactly guarding, checking, or inspecting—all customary duties of castle sentries—more lingering, as though waiting for someone. Even though the kingdom was at peace, usually the guards were occupied with *some* task: patrolling, practicing their drills on the parade ground, polishing armor, sharpening blades.

Is he awaiting the castellan? she wondered. The castellan and her father? With full royal confidence and authority, she walked up to the man and asked, "Are you one of the guards who apprehended the intruder?"

"Yes, my lady," he said, with a bow. "Me and Kilby."

"Show me," she said.

The man looked startled, confused even, but since her question clearly implied that the castellan had informed her about the prowler, there would be no reason she shouldn't be taken to where the stranger was being kept. The guard bowed again, explaining, "We found him at the far end of the garden during our first round of the morning, so we put him in the garden shed."

Her father and the castellan had said the intruder probably wasn't working for Prince Sheridan, but they didn't know for sure. She asked, "Is that secure enough to hold him?"

"There's not much to him," the guard said. "And, whatever his purpose, he's a bit inept. Knocked himself out."

That didn't sound good. That sounded as though the guards were bullying and maltreating someone whom she'd heard described as younger than her, scruffy, not right in the head, and with not much to him. "Knocked *himself* out?" she repeated.

"Truly," the man said, clearly seeing her distrust of his account. "We had done no more than take hold of his arm, and he tried to squirm away. Next thing we knew, we're still holding on to the empty sleeve of his ragged shirt, and his feet are sliding out from under him in the mud. And the next thing after *that*, he's flat on his back on the ground, any sense that he *might* have had knocked out of him. So we carried him to the shed. Kilby is standing guard outside."

"Fine," Amelia said. She could make a conclusive judgment once she actually talked with the prisoner. "Take me to him." She wanted to do this quickly, before her father could come out and tell her to stay away and leave this matter to the adults.

The guard hesitated, weighing the unusual request against the fact that it was the princess asking it. In the end he said, "Yes, my lady."

She hadn't been sure which shed the guard had been talking about, but as they walked, she realized it was the one she had been near last night when she'd gone out to the river's edge, precisely because she'd wanted to be alone. When, exactly, had he arrived, this person—never mind the young, ragged, and inept part—who was described as giving the appearance of being not right in the head? While she'd been there? Silently watching her? Because—if he *had* been by the river at the same time she was, she hadn't noticed him.

Of course, she hadn't seen that girl, either, not until she spoke—the one talking about wishes, and with what had looked, under the moonlight, like silver hair. Surely the guards hadn't taken hold of her, had they, mistaking her for a boy, a nothing-much-to-him boy? Amelia hadn't recognized her but had assumed she must belong to the castle, because otherwise she wouldn't have been there. And yet at least one person who didn't belong *had* been there.

Amelia remembered that she'd been unable to determine if the mysterious girl was very young or just short. *Could I have been mistaken about her gender?* she wondered. But, no, the child had definitely been a girl.

By then, they had reached the shed. A second guard was there—Kilby, apparently—sitting on the ground with his back against the door. As soon as he saw her, he jumped to his feet and bowed. She asked both of them, "Are you sure this is a boy you've captured and not a girl?"

Looking confused—there seemed to be a lot of that between the two of them—they assured her that it was definitely a boy, probably twelve or thirteen years old, skinny and ragged.

Amelia nodded. "Well, then, open the door."

One guard raised the bar that held the door from flapping in the wind, while the other stood ready just in case their prisoner planned to use the opportunity to try to escape.

The door opened . . .

. . . and there was no one there, neither boy nor girl.

Just a bony and rather raggedy rabbit, who blinked in the sunlight, then bolted out the door.

One of the guards stood by her, while the other entered the shed, poking at the coarse-cloth bags scattered on the floor, looking behind pots that were obviously much too small to hide anyone.

"You were supposed to be watching!" the one who had accompanied her shouted to the other. "How did you let him escape?"

"I didn't!" Kilby protested. "I been here the whole time. Nobody come out that door."

"So you saying you see him here?" the first guard demanded.

"Well, he must of got out another way, then." Kilby picked up a hoe and ran the handle along the bottom of the walls. "There must be a hole," he said.

But all three of them could see there wasn't.

The first guard started berating his partner, accusing him of having fallen asleep or of wandering off.

Amelia decided it was time for *her* to wander off. When her father arrived, her presence here could do nothing but complicate things. It wasn't as though Prince Sheridan was likely to jump out from behind the rosebushes at her. Intruder or not, she felt perfectly safe in the gardens.

She followed the winding paths, occasionally stopping to sniff at the fragrant blooms, hoping to quiet her churning mind.

She made it all the way back to the castle without seeing, hearing, or sensing anyone. But as she put her hand on the latch of the door that opened onto the ballroom, the same she had left by last night, she heard the crunch of a footstep behind her. Before she could turn, someone had one arm around her waist and the other around her neck, with his hand over her mouth so that she couldn't scream—his dirty, foul-smelling hand.

No, it was a dirty, foul-smelling cloth that someone was hold-ing over her face. Henbane: She recognized the thick, musty-sweet scent from her lessons with the botanist. He'd warned her to avoid the plant if she could, or use it very carefully only if she must. "A little will render your patient unconscious," he had said. "Just a little more will render him dead."

Assuming whoever had hold of her wanted to capture her and not kill her, did he know exactly what he was doing?

Amelia stopped struggling, to encourage her captor not to linger with that cloth at her nose and mouth. Her senses swirled dizzyingly, and the last thing she was aware of was her legs col-lapsing under her.

~ *Chapter 5* ~

Travels by Hop, Wing, and Wagon

TELMUND

Telmund ran out of the shed as fast as his bunny legs would take him, past the two guards who had captured him in his human form, past a surprised-looking princess—he could tell by her dress and bearing that she was a princess, even though he didn't recognize her.

He didn't have time to worry about the humans. He was more preoccupied with the way his bunny legs worked. As much as he had planned to run straight past the people, his legs had minds of their own. The front ones made him zig and zag, and the back ones periodically and unexpectedly propelled him to leap into the air, where he often both zigged and zagged, finding himself in an entirely unexpected place when he landed.

He supposed it was his bunny brain at work, tactics to avoid ending up as breakfast for some bigger and faster animal. Not that he expected there to be too many of those in the formal gardens of a royal family. As far as the humans went, even if they had plans for him that involved stewing, roasting, or pickling, he'd long ago lost sight of them, and he heard no sounds of pursuit.

Stop, Telmund ordered his legs. *There's no immediate danger.* The back pair gave one more half-hearted *sproing* into the air.

Was this the witch's idea of a joke? Turning him into a rabbit after giving him brief moments back in his own body? Telmund didn't find it funny. He tried not to let himself get too encouraged at the thought that it showed he *could* turn back.

Telmund realized that once his legs had stopped moving, his mouth had started. Without even knowing that he'd done it, he grabbed a blossom off a phlox plant and was eating it. Whatever he would have thought of it as a boy, his rabbit self was delighted.

Was it better to be a rat or a rabbit? A rabbit was bigger, so that meant not as many animals could swallow him in a single mouthful. That was good. And his eyesight as a rabbit was keener than it had been as a rat. On the other hand, how would he ever get *anyone* to know who he was? Even Wilmar would be hard to convince, since he would be on the lookout for a gray rat.

But meanwhile, was that an iris?

Telmund hopped across the path and chewed on the crunchy stem, which he somehow knew tasted just as delectable as the flower would.

Was his rabbit mouth any better suited than his rat mouth had been to human speech?

"Hello," Telmund said. "I'm Prince Telmund." Even given that his mouth was full of iris at the time, the sound that came from him couldn't be described as anything besides a very soft grunt.

Not having any idea where he was, the only way he could think to get home was to follow the river upstream. It would be slower traveling on land as a rabbit than it had been floating downstream as a rat. And he knew that not all the terrain the river had flowed through would be as hospitable as a royal garden.

Which way *was* the river?

He gave a couple more hops but found himself distracted by a patch of peonies. Why hadn't the cook at his father's castle ever served these things?

Telmund was so busy munching, he startled himself when his right hind leg thumped. *Now why did it do that?* he wondered. But even as he wondered, he was filled with dread. *Run!* his rabbit brain warned him. *Danger! Danger! Run!*

Which way?

Telmund stood on his hind legs to look over the peonies but found himself sniffing the air as much as he was looking.

Good thing. Because from behind him came the smell of . . .

His human brain failed him, but his rabbit brain supplied the picture of a cat.

Telmund leaped into the air and twisted to look behind.

Yes, definitely a cat. Big and orange. And crouched low to the ground, looking directly at him. Its legs flexed, about to spring.

Telmund took off, zigzagging and leaping.

The cat pursued.

It was bigger and faster than him, but Telmund's bunny antics made it hard for the cat to follow. Still, Telmund could hear the cat's paws striking the ground, alarmingly close, slapping at the plants and leaves underfoot. He was certain he felt the cat's breath on his backside, though surely that wasn't possible, not through his bunny fur. But he could smell the cat's breath, rank with dead meat. And that gave him a burst of speed.

There was a log serving as the border of one of the flower beds. Telmund raced toward that, seeing an indentation in the ground beneath the log. *Not nearly big enough*, Telmund's human brain calculated. *Yes, it is!* his bunny brain assured him.

Into the cavity Telmund ran.

The good news was that he fit. The bad news was that it was a dead end. Whatever had created the hole, it didn't go all the way under the log and exit to the other side. Telmund pivoted, ready to race out again.

But the cat was there, licking its lips.

The cat lay down in front of the hole. It reached a paw toward Telmund, claws extended.

Telmund pressed his back to the space where ground and log met, and ducked his head.

The claws touched his whiskers, but not enough to catch hold of him.

The cat hissed and scratched at the dirt.

Check the other side, Telmund mentally urged the cat. *See if you can get me that way.*

But the cat stayed where it was.

As though it had a mind of its own, Telmund's back leg thumped in alarm.

The cat continued to scratch away at the dirt.

Eventually, it would make the hole big enough to reach in.

Telmund tried to turn around again, to face the other way, so he could use his front paws to dig his way out under the log. But as soon as he started to move, he momentarily put himself closer to the cat.

The cat's claws raked through the fur on his front leg, not reaching through to the skin but proving that Telmund couldn't turn without getting seriously injured.

There was no way out of this predicament. He couldn't stop from crying out "Help!" No word came, but his rabbit throat gave voice to a piercing scream. His rabbit brain told him this was the sound a rabbit would make if mortally wounded.

And then, beyond all reasonable expectation, help came.

A pair of hands reached down and picked up the cat. "You," a girl's voice said, "must go away. I declare this a place of sanctuary."

The cat hissed and jumped from the girl's arms, but it didn't take up its place in front of the log. Instead it slinked away, as though that had been its intention all along.

The girl knelt down in front of the hole.

No, Telmund saw not a girl: a fairy. He knew fairies because his next-older brother, Frederic, was married to one. Besides, she had silver hair, and her wings were showing over her shoulders as she leaned forward to look at Telmund.

"Thank you," he said.

"You're welcome," she answered.

Telmund's nose twitched in surprise. "You can understand me?" He was so surprised that he didn't struggle against her as she placed her hands on either side of him and gently pulled him out.

"Of course. Fairies speak all the languages of animals. It's our job to protect animals."

Telmund wasn't sure if it was smart of him to admit it, but he said, "I'm not really a rabbit."

"Close enough," the fairy said. She stood, still cradling him in her arms. "Just as you were close enough to being a rat that I moved you off the path last night, so Princess Amelia didn't accidentally step on you after you crawled out of the river." She began walking.

"Are you going to bring me back to my own kingdom?" Telmund asked, his heart lifting with hope.

The fairy considered. "I don't see how that would help you as a rabbit. And you-as-an-animal is all I'm concerned with."

"I'm not always a rabbit," Telmund protested.

She nodded. "I can see the spell you're under. Every time you fall asleep, you'll wake up as something else. Every other time, it's your natural form."

"Oh," said Telmund. He was familiar with a lot of once-upon-a-time stories, but none of them had a spell like that. "So all I have to do is fall asleep, turn back to myself, and make it back home on my own."

"That might be one thing you could do," the fairy said.

"So where are you taking me?" Telmund asked.

"Here." They had come up behind a two-horse wagon loaded with sheaves of straw. There was a tarp on top, evidently to protect the straw in case of bad weather. One man was already sitting down at the reins, while a second man was just climbing on. The fairy approached from behind and didn't make a sound, so the men were unaware of her. She didn't need to lift the tarp, since it didn't reach all the way down in the back. From the top, the sheaves appeared to be piled randomly on the bed of the wagon. But from his rabbit's-eye view in back, Telmund could tell that the mound was carefully stacked, with the sheaves crisscrossing in a way to form a hollow. The fairy set Telmund into this hollow.

"Where is this wagon going?" Telmund asked her.

"Not a clue," she answered in a whisper. "But hopefully out of my territory, so you'll be someone else's problem."

The wagon jostled as the horses started walking.

The fairy gave a cheery wave, then turned and walked away.

Telmund considered jumping off and running after her, to try and explain to her that he was the brother of the human ambassador to the fairy court. She really should be nicer to him. But he suspected she wouldn't be impressed. And even though Telmund's mind told him the pair of horses weren't going all that fast, it *felt* pretty fast by rabbit standards.

Where were the men taking their wagonload of straw? Telmund knew that chances were equally good they'd bring him closer to—or farther from—his own Kingdom of Rosenmark.

In a story, being rescued by a fairy only to be abandoned on a wagon filled with straw, destination unknown, would be the start of an adventure. In a story, everything would eventually work out well—at least for a younger son. In a story, the hero always knew what to do next.

So should he jump or stay?

As a human, Telmund wouldn't have found the distance from the wagon bed to the ground to be high. Even for someone rabbit-sized, it shouldn't seem that daunting. But Telmund found out something he hadn't known until that very moment: Rabbits are afraid of heights.

Especially moving heights.

He couldn't bring himself to jump . . . He couldn't bring himself to jump . . . Then the wagon turned the corner of the castle, and he could no longer see the fairy girl.

They were on a cobblestone road. The wagon bounced and tipped and rattled alarmingly. Telmund hopped farther in, away from the edge. The sheaves of straw were stacked this way and that, but loosely, leaving what could almost be called a path leading deeper in.

Telmund sniffed in the direction of the front of the wagon. Something was in here besides the straw. His bunny brain sent him the picture of a human. Was he smelling the two men? He suspected they wouldn't smell as nice as this. He hopped farther in.

There, lying on the lowest layer of straw, with other sheaves stacked around and over to form a little straw cave, was the girl he'd glimpsed as he ran from the shed. A princess, he recalled thinking. The fairy had referred to a Princess Amelia almost stepping on him.

Was she dead?

Telmund hopped right up to her and saw that she was breathing.

So what was Princess Amelia doing, sleeping in a wagon full of straw? Surely she was not inclined to nap in strange places. Telmund suddenly noted that her wrists and ankles were bound by rope, and there was a gag over her mouth.

He moved in closer, his bunny nose sniffing. The scent he was tracking was strongest near her face. As a boy, he wouldn't have been able to say what he was smelling. His rabbit sense warned: *Not good! Stay away! Don't nibble! Danger!* His shared boy/rabbit brain told him the princess had been dosed with something. That meant this sleep was unnatural, and no doubt it wouldn't do him any good to try to rouse her.

The wagon creaked to a stop, and Telmund heard voices. Castle guards, he realized. They questioned the men, who were telling a story about having delivered pastries and prepared meats in fancy serving dishes for the royal festivities.

Lies, Telmund's nose told him. No food had been here.

The edge of the tarp was pulled back, admitting a little more light, but not much, into the heart of this straw cave. A couple sheaves shook as the guards poked at them, but the examination was hardly thorough. Telmund heard the guards wish the men a good day, and the wagon started to move again.

Telmund ran to the back edge. "No!" he cried. "They're making off with your princess! Stop them!" It came out *Grunt! Snuffle! Grunt!*

The wagon was still moving quite slowly. He *might* have been able to talk his bunny legs into jumping down onto the road.

But there was no way to tell anyone what he knew. And he couldn't leave the princess on her own—even if it *had* taken a not-very-friendly fairy's intervention to keep her from stepping on him. That wasn't the way heroes acted in stories, and it wasn't the way *he* would act.

But how could a rabbit help her? He didn't even have hands, much less a blade to cut through the ropes that held her.

There was nothing he could do about not having a blade.

But he would have hands the next time he woke up.

And, for now, he had teeth.

He set to work nibbling at the rope that held Amelia's hands together, then he nibbled through the one around her ankles.

The princess sighed in her sleep and curled into a more comfortable position.

After all that hard work, the chewing without eating, Telmund was ready for a nap.

AMELIA

The advantage of having studied with the royal botanist, besides knowing not to inhale henbane deeply, was that Amelia was aware the plant was likely to cause strange dreams and result in visions of things not really there.

So as her senses began once more to swirl close around her, Amelia was not unduly alarmed that the surface on which she was lying was swaying from side to side, rocking backward and forward, dipping and lifting. She'd never been on a boat but concluded that she was dreaming she was on an ocean-faring vessel. In her dream, she opened her eyes and found herself on the deck of a ship. It was night (was it supposed to be night?) and the sky was totally black. But it was also speckled with stars more bright and numerous and colorful than she had ever before seen from home. She was aware enough to wonder: Could stars really twinkle in jewel tones? She hadn't read that they did, but if not, that was a shame.

Whether it was from opening her dream eyes, or staring at the stars, or wondering about them, Amelia lost contact with the deck and began floating upward.

Yes, the stars really were like sparkly gems on black velvet. And that was almost enough to hold off the nagging wonder of how she'd gotten here.

Henbane, she remembered.

And rough hands holding her . . .

She'd been kidnapped! Had she escaped by flying?

Rolling over to face downward, she could see the ship she'd been on growing smaller and smaller. Tiny pirates stood by the railing, shaking their fists at her, and the pirates all looked like Prince Sheridan of Bittenhelm.

If only I could direct my flight . . ., Amelia thought. Whereupon her arms changed to wings—which were useful things to have if you were flying. The wind blew in her hair—she still had hair, as well as feathers—and she wondered if her maid, Constance, would be annoyed at the extra work involved with tending a feathered princess.

But then she was flying in shadow. And she wondered what it could be a shadow of, as she was so high in the sky. She looked up and saw another bird—an enormous creature whose wings blocked out the sun.

And then the gigantic bird began hurtling toward her. Closer . . . Closer . . . Its sharp talons reached toward her.

"Don't eat me!" she cried. "I'm not really a wren. I'm a princess!"

"I know," the bird of prey answered. From its beak came a carrion stench, and Amelia wondered if that was from other birds—or other princesses—it had eaten. And in the moment she looked from its talons to its face, she recognized Prince Sheridan.

Amelia woke with a start.

The light was dim, but she could see that she was not in the sky, nor on a boat. However, she was still being rocked and jostled, indications she was definitely moving. There was a stinging sensation at her wrists and ankles. She wasn't tied, but she suspected she may have been at some point. She was, however, gagged, which made no sense with her hands free to pull the cloth down. This wasn't the henbane-soaked rag or she'd be dead from so much of it. The cloth was dirty and dusty, and now the inside of her mouth tasted dirty and dusty, too.

And what was that all around her? She reached out a hand and felt the prickliness at the same time she recognized the smell. There were sheaves of straw piled all around her: not lying *on top of* her but over her, surrounding her, forming a tiny chamber of straw. She remembered a story her father had told when she'd been a small child. It involved a pig who built a house of straw. What had happened? Oh yes, a wolf came along, destroyed the house, and ate the pig. "But the clever, hardworking third pig survived," her father had rushed to say, skipping to the ending because she'd started crying.

And her parents wondered why she didn't like their stories.

Clearly, she wasn't in a pig's straw house. She was in a wagon—a wagon hauling straw.

But besides the scent of straw, there was something that smelled bad. Had some of the straw been fouled before being gathered up into bales? What she had smelled in her dream, she realized, hadn't been rotting meat. Rather, it reminded her of stagnant water, as when a flower vase escaped the servants' notice so that they didn't freshen the water every day. Some perfectly lovely flowers—carnations came to mind—would give off an abominable odor after only a day or so. It was a stench of rotting vegetation seemingly beyond all reason, and certainly beyond all proportion to such a delicate flower.

What had been packed with this straw that could account for the awful smell?

Because of the way the straw was stacked, there wasn't much light, but there was *some*. Amelia could make out something lying next to her. The henbane-soaked cloth that had been used to render her senseless?

She sat up, as much as she could in this confined space, and supported herself on an elbow to lean in closer. No. It was a rabbit, a sleeping rabbit—a *stinky* sleeping rabbit.

"Oh, rabbit," she said, covering her nose. "What have you gotten yourself into?"

From this slightly different perspective, she saw that there was a corridor of sorts leading to the back of the wagon, and that was where the majority of the light was coming from.

As bad as the rabbit smelled, now that her mind was clearing, she realized that wasn't her main problem. She had been kidnapped. She could only suppose this had been done under the orders of Prince Sheridan of Bittenhelm. No doubt she was being transported to him. How many men were driving this wagon? It had taken only one to grab her, but she estimated there were probably more. She needed to get away while they believed she was still under the influence of the henbane.

Amelia twisted herself around so that she was on hands and knees facing what had to be the back of the wagon.

She was not the sort of person who would intentionally kick a rabbit—even a smelly one—but as she moved, her foot brushed against the creature.

. . . And it changed, right before her eyes.

Its fur faded away.

Its ears shrank.

Everything else shifted shape and grew longer, bigger. Much bigger.

Person-sized.

In fact, the rabbit *was* now a person—and the only good thing to say about that was that he was not Prince Sheridan. Rabbits don't change into people, so obviously, Amelia wasn't as clearheaded as she'd thought, that she could look at a person and mistake him for a rabbit.

Unless she was now looking at a rabbit and mistaking him for a person . . .

But a person made more sense than a rabbit. This must be one of the prince's men, who'd been sent to wrest her from home and family. This one, no doubt, had been placed next to her in the wagon to guard her, to make sure she didn't escape once she awoke. The fact that he'd been watching her while she slept made her skin itch.

And no matter what his form, he still stank.

"Get away from me," she told him. Amelia wouldn't kick a rabbit, but she did feel free to kick at a kidnapper. She crawled to the edge of the wagon. It was a lot noisier out here, with the wood creaking and the wheels bouncing in and out of ruts. Over the tarp-covered dome of piled straw sheaves, she could see two more men sitting at the front, one holding reins and directing the horses. The other, improbably, was napping.

"Princess Amelia," hissed the youth she had mistaken for a rabbit. He grabbed hold of her arm. "Quiet," he warned. He crouched beside her at the edge of the wagon and glanced back toward his fellows. "We must escape."

Some kind of game? Or test?

Well, of course she'd want to escape.

But out here in the sunlight her head ached and the air shimmered and wavered, the way it does around a candle flame. The henbane was still affecting her mind, which would make escaping more difficult. They'd easily recapture her, and be on the alert.

No . . . he was taunting her.

Never mind that he looked much too young to be such a villain. That was what he was.

She kicked him again.

"Ow!" he complained, but still he kept his voice lowered. "I'm trying to help."

Sorry, no—she didn't believe that.

She shoved, and he toppled off the edge of the wagon and onto the road, headfirst.

He didn't get back up. Amelia hoped, in a fuzzy sort of way, that she hadn't killed him—even if he was a villain.

At least he didn't turn back into a rabbit, which would have made her feel sorry for him.

She presumed that eventually his compatriots would notice his absence and return for him.

Meanwhile, she wouldn't play his game and jump off in a bid to escape. He might well leap up and grab hold of her, for there was a good chance he was only pretending to have knocked himself out.

Something about that idea—someone knocking himself out— tickled at her uncooperative brain.

Where had she heard . . . ?

But she didn't know the sort of people who would knock themselves out, so the idea flew away.

Pretending or not, at least rabbit boy had taken his bad smell with him.

Amelia put her head down on her arms and fell back asleep.

Chapter 6

Complications

TELMUND

Telmund remembered being on the straw cart with Princess Amelia, who was being kidnapped. He remembered her wild and confused eyes. He remembered her kicking him—several times, as a matter of fact—and pushing him off the cart, even though he'd assured her he was there to rescue her. That was even more unfriendly than the fairy girl who had refused to help him get back home. At least *she* hadn't resorted to physical violence.

Being raised in a family of five boys, Telmund hadn't had much experience with princesses. But the ones in stories wouldn't have acted that way. *They* would have cooperated in their rescue— or at least not fought it.

His head ached. As far as he remembered, the princess hadn't kicked him there. Ribs and knees, definitely, which must mean his head hurt because . . .

He sighed. But he didn't open his eyes, afraid of what he might see.

She had pushed him off the cart. He remembered the sharp pain as his head hit the road. Probably the only thing that had stopped him from cracking his skull wide open was that this far from the castle, the road had gone from cobblestones to dirt.

Every time you fall asleep, the fairy had told him, *you'll wake up as something else.*

Telmund suspected, even with his eyes closed, that he was no longer in his human form.

What new treat did the witch's spell hold in store for him?

He opened his eyes. He was still on the dusty road. There was no sign of the cart carrying away the princess. Just ruts in the dirt to show that many carts traveled this way. He turned to look the way they had come. No glimpse of the castle the princess had been kidnapped from, not even way off in the distance.

Telmund moved his arms to make sure nothing was broken from his fall but also to see what kind of hands he had.

The arms didn't move forward very well—just enough to give him a view of brown feathers.

He didn't have arms at all—he had wings.

He cried out in frustration, and it was a scratchy, grating sound that came from his mouth. Or, rather, beak.

But maybe this wasn't so bad. As a bird, he could fly up in the air, get a sky view of the countryside. Rivers and forests and bad terrain would not be a delay but something to explore, to soar over, like moving your finger effortlessly over a map. How often had he watched powerful raptors gliding just that easily on a current of air? They'd plummet earthward to snatch up a meal of some small animal, only to take back to the sky with powerful beats of their mighty wings. He could be back in his father's kingdom in no time at all.

If he wanted.

But a new yearning pulled him in the opposite direction. In fact, he might not even go directly back, if flying was as much fun as he knew it would be. Of course, back home his parents would be worried about him, no doubt thinking he was still a rat, and probably fearful that he was a drowned rat.

However, given that they would already be fretting, one afternoon longer wouldn't make *that* much difference.

His mind fluttered here and there. Telmund would return when he was tired out. Then he'd find someplace on the castle grounds to go to sleep. Once he woke up, back in his human form, he could go to his parents and tell them what had happened to him. He could also tell them what had happened to the princess. A rescue party could be sent out to find her, and she'd be their problem, not his.

He was ashamed of the plan as soon as he thought it.

That sounded like the hard-hearted reasoning the fairy had used on *him*: Get rid of Telmund so she wouldn't have to deal with his problems.

The more honorable thing to do was to find the princess first, before returning home. Honorable, and more. It would be a worthy excuse, even an admirable one, should his mother ask, *Did you come directly home?*

I couldn't, he'd answer truthfully. *Because I knew that I'd be able to catch sight of the horse-drawn wagon more easily from the sky, that I'd find the princess with less trouble than any rescue party on foot ever could.*

He'd take note of where the princess was, then go home with that information.

I can do this, he thought, *AND it will be fun.*

What kind of bird was he, he wondered: Gyrfalcon? Peregrine? Hawk?

He looked down at his feet. Sharp toes were scratching at the dirt as though they had a mind of their own. They were big, but they didn't look like the mighty talons of one of the greater birds of prey.

So maybe he was a lesser bird: a merlin or an eagle or even an owl. It didn't make any difference, not really. He could be a raven and it would still be the same. He had wings; he could fly. And after he'd had his fill of flying, and helped save a princess along the way, his ordeal would be over.

Telmund flapped his wings. To go along with the not-mighty-talons, he had not-mighty-wings. Maybe he was a sparrow. No doubt the witch who'd bespelled him would have thought that a most entertaining progression: rat, rabbit, sparrow.

He turned his face to the sun. The not-mighty-wings lifted him into the air. The wind ruffled his feathers. Below him, the ground grew distant . . .

Well, not so much *distant* as *away* . . .

Well, not so much *away,* as it was beneath him, and he wasn't touching it.

Except he would be touching it in another moment: He was sinking rather than rising.

He reached the lower branch of one of the trees that grew by the side of the road.

There would be no soaring over the countryside for him.

He jumped from this only-slightly-higher-than-the-road vantage. And fluttered earthward.

What kind of bird could fly only about as high as a man was tall?

He cried out in frustration, but it came out sounding less like the angry screech he had intended, and more like a cluck.

He sighed, and it came out a very dispirited *Cock-a-doodle-doo*.

No doubt about it: He was a rooster.

Telmund scratched at the dirt while he thought.

Scratch-scratch-scratch.

There was no way he could catch up to the wagon carrying the princess, not as a chicken, because chickens were useless, except for eating.

Scratch-scratch-scratch.

He could try falling asleep, because then he would wake up as a human.

But by the time he fell asleep, dozed, and woke up, most likely the princess, the wagon, and the princess stealers would be long gone.

Scratch-scratch-scratch.

There was no way he could catch up to the wagon. Not as a chicken, because chickens were useless, except for eating.

Scratch-scratch-scratch.

He could try falling asleep . . .

Telmund heaved a sigh from the depths of his rooster chest. His thoughts were going around in circles, because . . .

Chickens were useless, except for eating.

Telmund wondered if the three gnats and a beetle that his scratching had uncovered might be distracting him, so he ate them.

His thinking did not grow noticeably clearer.

He scratched some more.

Scratch-scratch-scratch.

His choices were to chase after the princess as he was, or to take the time—however long that might call for—to sleep off his rooster form.

He forced himself to stop scratching. Human or chicken, it was just wrong to take a nap while someone he was supposed to be rescuing was in trouble.

He gave the ground one more scratch.

Ooo, there was a big, juicy grub.

Telmund gobbled that up and couldn't help delaying for a few more scratches in case there was another nearby.

Maybe there might be another over here . . .

. . . or here . . .

. . . or . . .

Stop it! Telmund ordered himself.

He started walking, as briskly as his little rooster feet would take him.

. . . With occasional stops for *a little* scratching.

AMELIA

Amelia was reluctant to open her eyes. The last time she'd thought she was ready, the world hadn't made sense. She'd had trouble determining what was real, and what was dreaming, and what was awake-but-still-not-real.

Someone had stolen her away from home. That seemed so wildly improbable in a bad-dream sort of way, normally she would be inclined to dismiss the whole idea. But it was the single thing she was most sure of: the rough hands taking hold of her, pressing a cloth soaked in henbane over her face. And henbane explained why her mind was so sluggish, her thoughts only half-formed and slippery.

So the kidnapping had actually happened.

What else was real?

She was being conveyed in a wagon—she could tell by the way the wheels jostled when they hit ruts and holes in the road, and by the creaking of the boards, and by the dusty, nose-scratching smell of straw.

As for the pirates, and the flying, and the people who were sometimes people and sometimes rabbits, that was henbane haziness.

Amelia forced herself to open her eyes. Despite the lurching of the wagon, she was feeling steadier than before. Sheaves of straw crisscrossed above her. At first glance the stacking looked random—probably even more so from an overhead view—but clearly, someone had been meticulous about the arrangement.

Amelia was perfectly concealed, but enough space had been left around her so she could breathe. Light was coming in from what her senses told her was the back of the wagon, so it was still day. Or day again.

Don't panic, she told herself. *Don't exaggerate your problems.*

Henbane would knock someone out for the better portion of a day, but this had to still be the same day. The opening Amelia could see through the bundles of straw wasn't big, but she could glimpse trees. She was being carried through a wooded area.

That didn't help her get her bearings. Travel far enough from Pastonia in any direction and there would be woods.

No doubt it was late afternoon by now. Her parents could be oblivious at times, but surely they'd have noticed her absence. On the other hand, they wouldn't have a clue as to *what* had happened. They'd call for the castle to be searched, and the garden, probably conjecturing that she'd taken ill or fallen or injured herself.

The last thing she needed to do was to lie here letting her mind wander. Now was the time for action, not woolgathering as though she were safely home on a rainy nothing-to-do morning. Amelia was not helpless, and she shouldn't assume rescue was on its way.

This wasn't *exactly* what all her training in leadership and sciences and languages had prepared her for, but whatever was going on, she needed to escape her captors. The sooner the better.

But she'd only just gotten up onto her hands and knees when she heard something through the piled straw. From the front of the wagon, a gruff voice said, "Whoa," and the wagon creaked and slowed.

Had the fact that she was awake been discovered? Had she accidentally brushed against the sheaves above her, causing them to shift and betray that she was moving?

No, she assured herself. If that had happened, she would have felt her back touch the straw. No, she couldn't see her captors, and they couldn't see her. Only the unhappiest of circumstances had brought her to her senses just when it was too late to jump out of the wagon undetected.

She heard voices, male voices—three of them. Two, she estimated, came from the front of the wagon, the third from just a bit farther away. The men who had seized her were meeting up with someone new.

Amelia bit back her instinct to cry out for help. The third man might not be a well-met potential rescuer. If that was the case, the smartest tactic was not to give away that she was awake and listening. And able to resist.

In fact, the way the men were greeting one another indicated they were acquaintances. "Hey, Jud," called one of the men on the straw wagon.

"Willum," the new man greeted him. "Boyce."

They knew one another. So, not help for her. Help for her abductors. But the good news was that the two had spoken in the accents of common workingmen. And nobody had said, *Hey, Prince Sheridan*. For who else besides Prince Sheridan could be behind this? The longer Amelia avoided *him*, the better.

"Took your time," chided the gravelly voice of the person *not* on the wagon—the newcomer, Jud. "I was beginning to wonder iffen you'd-a got lost on the way."

"Yeah, well," said the second of the wagon men—disproving in two words any lingering doubts that *he* might be the prince—"she was already up and about, and we had to wait for her to get back to the castle."

"I di'n't think no princess would be up that early," the first man said. "Iffen I was royalty, *I* wouldn't get up no earlier than I had to."

"Well, Prince Sheridan ain't no slug neither," the second man said. "Shows how much *you* know."

And there she had it: These men *did* work for Prince Sheridan.

"She still asleep?" asked Jud.

"Haven't heard a peep from her," the second man said.

Very quietly, Amelia lowered herself back to the floor of the wagon. She closed her eyes and tried to breathe deeply and regularly, even as the men pulled away first the tarp covering, then the sheaves of straw.

Jud, the gravelly voiced one who was seeing her for the first time, said, "This is what all the fuss is about? I'd-a thought she must of been a real beauty. This'un ain't that much to look at."

It's one thing to have come to terms with yourself that you aren't particularly pretty. After all, beauty isn't an essential virtue to being a good ruler. But it's quite another thing to have someone say to your face, or at least to the top of your head, that you aren't attractive—even if the someone speaking is the kind of someone who would sneak into your parents' garden and steal you away by force. Princess Amelia let the words roll over her, forcing herself not to let any feelings of hurt or insult show in her pretending-to-be-asleep expression.

Unexpectedly, the better-spoken of the three men came to her defense. Sort of. "If Prince Sheridan wanted to marry someone with three eyes and two noses and a mouth on the back of her head, that's none of our business."

Marry? Amelia couldn't help a startled gasp, but she quickly disguised it as a snore. She stirred herself, as though settling into a more comfortable position.

"And she's younger'n I'd-a thought, too," said Jud, seemingly determined to find fault with her.

This time the first of the two wagon men spoke, clearly intent on playing up the second: "Yeah, and iffen Prince Sheridan wanted to marry someone with two eyes and three noses . . . No, wait, three noses and two eyes . . . No. Iffen he wanted—"

"Shut up, Boyce," said the man Amelia was already beginning to think of as the leader. "Dunderhead."

Sure enough, his companion was properly chastened. "Yes, Willum," he mumbled, "I was just—"

"Nobody cares," Willum growled.

Jud continued, "And I was just sayin' she seems like a kid."

"Iffen you don't have the stomach for this," said the man named Boyce, "maybe Willum needs to keep *me* with him and leave *you* with the straw wagon."

What? They met up, but they weren't staying together?

"Nay, Boyce," said Willum, "you dolt. One of us as was at the castle needs to stay with this wagon, just in case anyone that saw us back there comes upon you. What would they say if they saw the same wagon but with a different driver?"

"They'd say this plan is too confusing," Boyce grumbled.

Amelia suspected so, too, but Willum argued with him.

"Nay," he said. "The plan is fine. *You're* the only one as is confused."

"Well, come to that . . ." Jud started to admit.

But Willum talked over him. "I'll join Jud in the cart. Boyce stays on in the wagon. Boyce, if anyone asks, we had a falling-out over division of wages, and you left me behind on the road and you don't know where I got to. Jud, you leave any soft thoughts behind you."

"Ain't got no soft thoughts," Jud said in his gravelly voice. "Just sayin', was all."

"Hey!" said the one who was going to be left behind—Boyce. "She done got out of her bindings!"

Amelia felt someone jump into the wagon.

Breathe deep. Breathe steady.

"Nay," she heard Willum say from right next to her. "This been chewed, not untied. Must be rats." He kicked at the bundles of straw.

Rats? Could it have been a rat in here with her earlier? Amelia wondered. But how could she ever have mistaken a rat for a rabbit, never mind a person? She worked on not tensing at the thought that Willum's kick might send rats scurrying.

"Should you dose her again?" Jud asked.

Amelia was aware of Willum leaning in even closer over her. He snapped his fingers in her face.

Steady, calm breaths.

"Nay," said Willum, using what was apparently his favorite word. "She still be out. We don't want to take no chances. Prince Sheridan wants his bride alive. Here, Jud, help me lift her."

Her only chance for escape later was to make them believe she was asleep now.

One man took her by her shoulders, the other by her ankles. They lifted her up off the bed of the straw wagon. She peeked one eye open ever so slightly and saw that they were carrying her to a smaller second wagon. A cart, really.

Why? she wondered. She still didn't fully understand the men's plan. Was it more convoluted and complicated than it needed to be, or were the lingering effects of the henbane slowing down her ability to follow?

They placed her in a sitting position on the wagon seat. Amelia let herself slump and one of the men held her to keep her from sliding down.

"Where's that bundle of clothes?" Willum asked. Then, "Here, help me put this dress on her."

Amelia kept her eyes closed for the moment, but if they were going to be changing her clothes, she might have to take her chances now after all.

But they made no move to take off what she was wearing. They only slipped a coarse-woven gown over her own clothes. *Deadweight*, Amelia reminded herself, keeping her arms floppy

86

and her body saggy. One good lady's maid could have dealt with this a lot more handily than the three men, who struggled mightily.

"Anybody looks, they'll still recognize her," Jud protested. "Should we cut off her hair?"

"Prince Sheridan didn't authorize no such thing, you twit," Willum said. "Use this."

Someone tied some sort of kerchief around her head, evidently hiding her hair.

"And the cap attached to the fringe of red hair is for me," Willum said, "in case we run into anyone we saw on our way out."

"How we goin' to 'splain a sleepin' girl?" Jud complained.

One of the men leaned forward and touched her face with gritty fingers. She might or might not have twitched. But fortunately, before she gave herself away entirely, Amelia recognized the smell of strawberry. Maybe mixed with currants. The man was dabbing a sticky berry paste on her cheeks and throat.

Calm, Amelia told herself. *Steady. Breaths.* They were just trying to conceal her identity.

She gave another sleepy snort as the chunky mixture slid and dripped, tickling and leaving itchy paths across her cheeks, down behind her ears and around onto the back of her neck, and into her hair. It would, she knew, eventually attract flies. And bees.

Willum said, "Meet your sister, by name of Girly. She got some sort of pox, and we're bringing her to her grandmam. We hope we make it in time."

Girly? What kind of name was that? The pox part was clever enough, but didn't these men have any imagination at all?

"There," Willum said, evidently satisfied with his handiwork. "Now let's get moving so's we're headed toward the castle."

What? Amelia thought. *Why?*

Luckily, Jud had the same question. "Why're we doin' that, agin?"

Willum sighed. "How am I ever supposed to get anything done when I got to work with lackwits?" Slowly and carefully he explained, "They're likely to not even notice us as they'll think whoever's got the princess has got to be heading away. *Boyce* will be the one moving away—but he won't have no princess with him."

Jud grunted.

Meanwhile, Amelia wanted to cheer. They were going to be traveling back toward home? She couldn't believe her luck. She didn't need to escape and make her way back. All she had to do was keep on pretending to sleep, and her captors would return her.

But then Willum said, "But that daubin' on her face come close to wakin' her, so you're prob'ly right about dosin' her agin."

And before she could even open her eyes, much less make a break for it, she was once again inhaling henbane.

As her thoughts dissolved into a thousand fireflies that scattered into the night sky of her mind, she was aware of the man named Jud asking, "What if you give her too much and she dies?"

Willum answered without hesitation—or maybe it was a month or two later. "Then we won't return to Prince Sheridan."

Chapter 7

From Bad to Worse

TELMUND

Telmund sprinted down the road as fast as his drumsticks allowed. He did his chicken flap and flutter. He rooster-strutted. He stopped—only occasionally—to scratch at the dirt. What he did not do was turn back to see how far he'd come, because he suspected that would be disheartening. Although enough time had passed that by now it was late afternoon, he was afraid that he might still be able to see the spot from which he'd started not far off in the distance.

Perhaps now might be the time to try and sleep. He was certainly tired of walking, and it wouldn't take him long to drift off.

He shook his head to clear it, setting his wattles flapping. What was that he was hearing? He couldn't make out the sound. He wasn't even sure it *was* a sound. Was it a feeling that he was getting through the soles of his feet? (*Do* roosters have soles of feet?) Or were his feet tingling from so much walking?

But in another moment, he realized it was both a sound and a feeling.

A cart was approaching, coming at him from the direction he was heading.

Too bad. Had it been going the other way, he might have tried jumping on.

It was a simple open cart, carrying barrels and pulled by one tired-looking gray horse. Three people sat on the seat, farmers or lowly tradesmen by their clothing. Two men—one with shockingly red hair—and a woman who sat in between with her head resting against the shoulder of one of them. She was apparently more tired than the horse, for as they approached, Telmund could see she was sleeping. Also drooling a little bit.

Instinctively, Telmund had moved to the side of the road, but the man who held the reins saw him and pulled the horse to a stop.

"Chicken," he announced in a gravelly voice to Red-hair.

"Yeah?" the other man answered.

"Catch it, an we'll have dinner."

Did everything *always* have to go from bad to worse?

Telmund flutter-ran away from the road.

From behind him, he heard Red say, "I've got Her Royal Highness resting on my shoulder. *You* catch the chicken."

Telmund put on a burst of speed, but it didn't help: He could hear the footsteps of the man gaining. Telmund ran to the nearest tree, then tried to fly up to the lowest branch. He fell short, by quite a bit. Flung himself up into the air again. Still didn't get high enough. He turned, hoping to find a tree with lower branches, and ran right into the waiting man's hands.

"Got 'im!" Gravel-voice called back to Red, holding Telmund so that he couldn't flap his wings.

Telmund pecked at the man's hands, but despite crying "Ouch! Ouch! Ouch!" the man didn't let go.

"Should I wring its neck now?" Gravel-voice asked as he walked back to the cart, "or will it taste better iffen we wait to kill it till right afore we eat it?"

The man still in the cart was making a face. "Neither," he said. "There's something wrong with that chicken."

"What?" his captor demanded, clearly not wanting to give up on his dinner.

"Don't know. But you want to eat something smells that bad?"

The one who had hold of him sniffed. "I don't know," he said dubiously and maybe a little bit hungrily. "It's not that bad."

Yes, it is! Telmund thought at the man. He gave a series of twitches to reinforce the thought of disease, but the man may well have taken these movements as more attempts to escape. *I'm diseased! You'll catch something! Put me down!*

Almost as though he'd read Telmund's mind, Red echoed Telmund's thought. "Put it down, you pudding head," he said. "And get back in the cart. It's not worth the risk of eating something sick. We got provisions."

"Dry and stale," his captor sulked. But he must have been persuaded because he asked, "Should I wring its neck so it don't spread whatever it's got?"

No! Telmund mentally shrieked at him.

"I don't care." The man removed his cap to wipe his sweaty brow, and his red hair came off with the cap. "Just get in the cart, Jud. We got miles to cover tonight, and we don't want to keep Prince Sheridan waiting tomorrow."

Telmund managed to rake his taloned foot across the arm of the man named Jud, causing his grip to loosen enough that Telmund was able to wriggle free.

Jud kicked, but Telmund fluttered out of his range.

But not away entirely.

Even though he feared for his life, his rooster ears had quivered at the sound of a familiar name.

Prince Sheridan, he knew, was from a neighboring kingdom. Rittenhelm, maybe? Dittenheim? Something like that. Telmund's family—those who interested themselves with affairs of state— didn't like the man and considered him a political disaster waiting to happen. What could Prince Sheridan have to do with these men?

. . . and with the sleeping woman on the seat between them?

Red had called her "Her Royal Highness." Telmund had taken that as sarcasm, the kind of thing someone might say about another who wasn't working as hard as she should have been.

But now he took a better look. The woman was wearing a dirty, ugly, patched dress of coarse weave. It was so very baggy that it couldn't have been her own. She had some kind of cloth covering most of her hair, but what hung beneath the frayed edge was the right color for Princess Amelia. And, now that he was looking more closely, she wasn't a woman after all. She was a girl. A girl Telmund had seen sleeping once before—in the back of the straw wagon. But what had happened to her? Her face was flushed with what had to be the nastiest fever ever, coupled with vile bumps and pustules that oozed and . . .

No, wait . . . Telmund's chicken senses weren't very discerning, but that was fruit he was smelling. The princess had dried smears of—strawberry maybe?—on her face. A disguise?

But that made no sense. Why would her captors have switched the wagon for a cart and headed back *toward* the castle at Pastonia?

Except, of course, that it *did* make a certain kind of sense.

Once people realized the princess had been kidnapped, anyone looking for her would assume she was being taken away. That meant they'd be closely checking any carts or wagons heading out from the castle. They would scarcely give a second glance to those approaching. It was the kind of subterfuge used in adventure stories.

Good luck at last! Telmund didn't need to look for the princess—he'd found her!

The gravel-voiced man called Jud took several steps in Telmund's direction.

"Jud, you oaf!" his accomplice in the cart warned. "I'm gonna leave without you!"

"Aw, Willum," Jud complained, but he climbed back onto the cart.

Telmund took a flying leap for the back, where the barrels were.

But Jud had taken up the reins and snapped them, and the horse jerked into motion, yanking the cart away from where it had been a moment before.

Telmund missed the edge of the cart.

He ran after it, but his rooster legs weren't even as long as his human foot. The farther he ran, the farther ahead the cart pulled.

He stamped his rooster feet in exasperation.

Telmund was so busy being frustrated and furious he didn't hear the person coming up behind him. He was only aware of the danger when hands grabbed hold of him.

"Look, Pa!" a boy's voice called. "I caught 'im!"

"Well done!" a second voice cheered.

But Telmund didn't see either one of his new captors, for someone slipped a sack over his head.

"We gonna eat 'im tonight?" the younger voice asked.

What was this with everyone wanting to eat him? Telmund wondered if it was God saying to him, *Tell ME the only thing chickens are good for is eating. I spent time creating them, you know, same as I created you.*

"Naw," the father said. "I'm thinking on a plan. This be a chicken *rooster.* We'll borrow a chicken *hen* from Widow Nan, and we can start our own chicken flock. There be an old coop your ma used to tend, back behind the house. Carry that thing on home, and we'll put 'im in that."

Telmund bounced back and forth in the sack on the boy's bony shoulder blades as father and son started walking.

"But, Pa," the boy said. "Widow Nan don't like us. She won't never lend us no hen."

"Well," the father said, "we'll just have to borrow it without telling."

Fall asleep, fall asleep, Telmund ordered himself. He had just started to become interested in *girls*; the last thing he needed was girl chickens.

But it was impossible to drift off with all the bouncing.

Eventually, the sack was dropped to the ground.

"Here we go," the father said.

"It don't look too sturdy," the boy said.

"Just needs a bit of fixing up. Do we have a hammer?"

"Don't think so. Will a rock do?"

Telmund heard some hammering. Some snapping of wood. Some cursing. Some more hammering.

Eventually, the sack was picked up again, held upside down, and shaken.

Telmund fell into a wooden cage that was only about twice as big as he was. The lid came down with a thud, and the father hammered that closed.

The boy—he looked to be a year or two older than Telmund himself—peered through the slats. The young man's nose twitched. "Chickens supposed to smell like that?" he asked.

Diseased! Telmund thought at him. *With something deadly and highly contagious!* He flopped his head to one side and began walking in circles in his cage.

The father sniffed in Telmund's direction, then picked up the sack the two had carried him in. "We're just smelling them rutabagas we had stored in here that turned bad."

The boy nodded. "What's he eat?" he asked.

The father scratched his head. "I think he'll feed hisself on what he finds in the yard," he said. "See, that circling around he's doing means he's looking for food now. Once we get the hen, they'll be company for each other and won't wander off during the day."

"Will we get to eat 'im eventually?" the boy asked.

"Eventually," the father assured him.

The two of them walked into a peasants' house made of twigs and mud that Telmund could see beyond the bare yard.

He tried to squeeze himself between the slats, but they were too close together. He tried kicking at the slats, but they were too firmly nailed in. He tried jumping up against the ceiling of the cage, but the roof was too heavy to budge.

Telmund sighed.

He suspected a fox wouldn't have trouble crushing the flimsy structure. That was one more thing to worry about.

How do roosters sleep? he wondered. Lying down just felt wrong.

In the end, he tucked his head under his wing and hoped he would wake up before morning.

And before any foxes sniffed him out.

AMELIA
❧

Amelia's thoughts were jumbled and bouncing about like marbles in a sack. She saw several contradictory things all at once. Prince Sheridan was tying ropes to her wrists and ankles, four different ropes, each attached to a stick. He spoke with the voice of his henchman Jud. "What if them rats come back and chew through *these* while we be sleepin'?"

And he answered himself in Willum's scornful voice. "Those rats was in the other wagon, mush-for-brains."

Then Prince Sheridan stood, and he was very, very tall. So tall that the top of Amelia's head didn't even come as high as his knees. He loomed over Amelia. Sticks in his hand, he pulled up her right foot, then her left. Right, left, right, left: He had her walk in a circle like a puppet. At the same time Amelia knew she was still lying down on the ground. Outside. Almost—though not quite—asleep.

Even though he still controlled the movement of her feet from above, he also was standing in front of her, normal-sized.

The Prince Sheridan above tugged on the rope attached to one of her wrists, moving one of her hands into one of the waiting Prince Sheridan's hands. The other he placed on his shoulder. Right foot, left foot, around and around her parents' ballroom she danced with Prince Sheridan.

I don't want to dance! Amelia screamed. But her voice had no sound, and she had no control of her dancing self.

Everyone in attendance in the ballroom wore Prince Sheridan's face—and each section of the room clapped each time she and the prince passed.

And all the while the unseen Jud and Willum bickered in the background, first about dinner. ("We should of risked the chicken," Jud whined.) Then about whether they should put the blanket over her as Prince Sheridan would have wanted—even though she was sticky with fruit compote. (Which, Willum smugly pointed out, *had* helped get them past the castle guards searching for the missing princess, just as he'd said.) Or if one of them should take the blanket since she was, after all, asleep and would never know . . .

Chapter 8

Escape

TELMUND

Some nighttime predator—perhaps a fox or weasel, or maybe even an owl—landed with a thud on the roof of the chicken coop where Telmund slept with his beak tucked under his wing.

The noise startled him awake. And the awakening transformed him into his human shape . . .

Which was much too big for his cramped cage.

The sudden change sent his feet shooting out against the slats of the door, splintering the wood. His arms flew wide and slammed into the sides of the coop, while his head crashed against the back wall, all of which reduced the chicken coop to broken shards.

The force of the blows frightened away the creature that had come to investigate the newly inhabited coop.

But it also knocked Telmund senseless.

After he came to, but before he opened his eyes, Telmund's nose twitched. A fascinating stew of scents tickled his nostrils. There was the delicate aroma of river water, in which fish such as bream, pickerel, and minnows had swum, as well as ducks, geese, and small rodents.

This was overlaid by the tart tang of rotting vegetation—mainly alder, including leaves, wood, and bark, indicating a whole decaying tree—but also decomposing canary grass, horsetail, fennel pondweed, moss, and algae.

Distinct from, but no less interesting than, the watery smells was a piquant whiff that came from straw that had been out in the weather for at least a year and had begun to molder. The straw was peppered with eggshells and chicken droppings from both hens and roosters—most of it also more than a year old.

And then there was the fragrance of wood, which had been recently handled by humans.

Most intriguing was a hint of weasel, both strong because the creature had passed by recently but also thin because he (Telmund could tell it was a he-weasel) had lingered only for a moment.

Telmund sniffed again. The weasel had been startled away. But Telmund smelled nothing dangerous nearby. By the scent it had left behind, he could tell the weasel was a youngling, probably about three months or so, only recently out of its nest and away from its family. It was probably more skittery now than it would be later in its life.

However, the strongest smell of all, though least interesting and not at all alarming, was the scent of dog. This scent was totally familiar, because it was himself.

Telmund yipped, startled by the realization that he was a dog.

He'd just been a chicken! Had he skipped a turn as a human?

The soreness of his head and limbs, and the devastation of the chicken coop around him, hinted that he *had* been his own self, but only very briefly.

He howled his frustration to the moon.

Off in the distance—Telmund could tell exactly how many footsteps it would take to get there—another dog answered his distressed call, an assurance carried on the night wind that tomorrow would be another day, and probably a better one.

It's a sad state of affairs, Telmund mused, *when you're reduced to taking comfort from a dog you've never even met.*

Stop feeling sorry for yourself, he commanded. There was nothing that could make up for having squandered a turn as a human, but being a dog was better than being a chicken.

He scratched his ear with his hind leg, then marked the chicken coop as his territory. (He didn't *want* the chicken coop, but it was his by virtue of his being there.)

It was still dark out. His doggy sense told him the night wasn't yet half over. But he didn't need light to find the trail he was looking for: the path taken by the farmer and his son, carrying him as a chicken from the road. His nose told him exactly which way they had come.

He took off at a loping run. The trail was so fresh he didn't even need to pause to sniff the earth.

The road wasn't far at all. Once there, Telmund sniffed both ground and air. Many carts and wagons and walkers had passed this way, but he was able to single out the scent that he wanted as surely as a weaver would be able to pick a gold thread from among an assortment of blues and reds and yellows. The trail Telmund wanted smelled of princess and ruffians and strawberries.

His tail wagged in joy. He marked the spot on the road, simply to share his joy—then he began running.

As a dog, he was able to run faster than he could have as a boy, and he had greater stamina. In no time at all, he passed the spot where Princess Amelia had pushed him out of the wagon when it had been headed in the opposite direction. It was a bit disconcerting to catch hold of his human scent.

He'd be human again, he assured himself. His dog self told him that this was a shame, but it couldn't be helped.

A rabbit dove into the tall grass by the side of the road, and Telmund veered off to chase after it. *I was a rabbit, once*, he told himself, but the memory didn't stop him. Neither did the thought that he had more pressing business: to rescue a princess. *Surely she can wait until after I catch the rabbit*, Telmund told himself, but by then the rabbit had found one of the holes to its warren and disappeared underground.

Telmund scratched at the entrance, but he knew this was a losing battle. He marked the area to warn off any other passing dogs, just in case he remained a dog long enough to come back when he had more time.

Back to the road he went, and ran and ran.

Eventually, still in the dark of night, he came to the environs of the castle where the princess lived. Lights were on, and people were roaming the streets, calling the princess's name as though she might simply be lost, rather than stolen away.

Some of the searchers had dogs, and that was a distraction, as Telmund and the dogs made one another's acquaintance, sniffing at backsides and marking territory. *I'm sticking my nose in other dogs' private parts*, Telmund thought. The idea would have been disagreeable except for all the information he was learning about each dog. Most of the dogs were friendly, except one supremely full-of-himself hound who yipped a warning to stay away because his master was the king, and that made him more important than any other dog, even if they were bigger or better trackers.

Telmund left a "nobody-cares" puddle where that hound would have to walk through it, but he regretted it almost right away when he spotted a man who had to be the king. Telmund could tell by the respectful way people addressed him, just as most of the castle dogs walked respectfully around the unsociable hound. The king looked so sad, and Telmund remembered that it was his daughter everyone was looking for.

He wondered if his own father looked as sad for missing *him*.

Telmund gave a cheer-up *yip!* then kept on running. There were people and dogs searching at this end of town, too, but after a while Telmund was once again alone on the road, following the trail of the horse-drawn cart that carried the princess. He could tell it was the right cart because he recognized the scent of the horse—female, quite elderly, and with a little bit of a digestive problem—as well as the distinct smell of that particular wagon, the two men in it, and the strawberry-daubed princess.

Dawn was not too long away when Telmund caught the bubbly scent of a running river. He hoped the men who had the princess hadn't crossed the water. If they had, his only hope was that they'd gone straight across. Otherwise, it would be hard to know whether they had gone upriver or down. He would have to search in both directions and on either bank. He supposed that they were making for Prince Sheridan's kingdom, but Telmund's sense of geography was not all it should have been.

Still, before he came to the river, the trail scent became very strong indeed.

The horse that had been pulling the cart was on this side of the water, tethered beneath some trees. And there was the cart.

Telmund spotted three lumps on the ground, all asleep: two men and one princess still bearing bits of berries stuck to her face.

He knew it was her, but he sniffed her all over, because dogs like to be sure.

She was lying beneath a too-short, too-thin blanket. Telmund grabbed one corner with his teeth to uncover her, and this revealed that her wrists were tied together. So were her ankles.

Although his doggy brain protested, Telmund had to admit that his rabbit teeth had been better suited to gnawing through rope.

Maybe, his doggy brain conceded. *But I can still do it.*

AMELIA

Amelia woke up to alarming sounds close by—growly, moist, gnawing sounds—and the feeling that something was slobbering on her hands.

If something was eating her, she tried to reassure herself that surely she would have felt it before hearing it.

She opened her eyes.

The nighttime sky was just beginning to turn pink from dawn, so it was hard to see what was crouched beside her. Not one of Prince Sheridan's men—so that was good.

Or maybe not. Was it a wolf?

The creature heard the little squeal that escaped from her throat. It lifted its massive head and slavering jaws away from her hands and toward her face.

Her own head, which had felt so full of stuffing for the past day, picked this awful moment to have cleared, and she knew for a fact she was not seeing some henbane apparition.

This was no time for pretending to still be asleep in order to try to fool her captors.

But even as she inhaled to scream for help, the beast leaned in close—

—and licked her cheek.

That was so unwolflike a gesture that Amelia let the air out of her lungs in a silent sigh.

Dog, she realized.

Once she saw that, her estimation of its size—as well as its ferocity—diminished.

Can dogs smile? She wasn't sure, but this one certainly looked friendly, with its head cocked to one side, one ear up, the other down, and its tongue hanging out.

Could it be one of her father's hounds? She didn't know them all, but this one didn't look the least bit familiar.

It smelled familiar, however.

Was that stagnant-water odor a lingering effect of the henbane? She remembered smelling it in the straw wagon as she was coming around yesterday. The royal botanist had not mentioned henbane having such an effect, but surely this dog hadn't been in the wagon yesterday, or the men would have noticed it. And friendly as it seemed, it hadn't followed all day yesterday. Had it?

Not that she had any right to be pointing fingers at smelly creatures. The dress the men had slipped over her own had not been clean to begin with, and the berry mixture they'd smeared on her face as part of her "disguise" added a peculiar fruity scent that overlaid but did not diminish the dress's combination of sweat and dirt. She was itchy and sticky, too.

The dog, however, didn't seem to mind her unprincesslike state. It leaned in and gave her face another wet lick—was the creature friendly or was it simply enjoying the crusted remnants of fruit?—then it went back to gnawing at something near her hands.

Her rope bindings, she realized. And it wasn't that the dog was simply intent on chewing on the rope for some unknowable doggy reason, because it was carefully avoiding making contact with her skin. Somehow this dog gave every appearance of knowing she was in trouble, and in fact, it seemed determined to rescue her.

She felt a strand of the rope give way. The bindings loosened, but not enough to wriggle her hands free.

The dog nudged her side with its muzzle, perhaps telling her to have patience, then resumed chewing.

Although her wrists were still right up against each other, Amelia strained to pull her hands as far apart as she could—both an instinct to avoid the dog's teeth and to get the most out of any weakness in the rope.

Another strand came apart, and this time Amelia's wrists separated just the tiniest bit.

The dog whimpered in frustration.

"Easy, girl," Amelia urged in a whisper.

The dog reversed the upright ear and the floppy ear and looked at her with an expression that could only be interpreted as disapproval.

"Or boy," Amelia corrected. The nighttime shadows were still too deep to see details, and in any case, Amelia wasn't certain that a princess should be looking.

Apparently satisfied, the dog resumed tearing at the rope.

Finally her wrists sprang apart, and the rope dangled loosely.

The dog moved to her feet, but Amelia sat up and whispered, "Let me just pick at the knot."

Her captors were not careful people—evidenced by the fact that they were both sleeping, with neither set to watch—and the knot was not a complicated one. In just a few moments, Amelia kicked the rope off her legs. She paused long enough to give the dog a quick pat on the head, then she tugged off the dress with which the men had covered her own simple but still aristocratic gown.

She noted that the dog had sat back on its—*his*, apparently—haunches and was watching, clearly interested.

She bunched up the dress, then placed it under the blanket the men had provided for her. This couldn't fool anyone for long, but she hoped that, to someone just glancing in this direction, it would appear she was still here and asleep. It might gain her a moment or two.

She looked where the men lay sleeping. Amelia was not the kind of person who could take up a rock and crack somebody over the head. Even if she could bring herself to do it, there was no way she could incapacitate both men at once. Her best option was to flee as quickly as possible, knowing that they could bestir themselves at any moment.

The dog was on his feet, quivering in anticipation.

Because of the river, and because of her studies, she knew exactly where she was in relation to both her own Kingdom of Pastonia (upstream) and Prince Sheridan's Bittenhelm (across the water and downstream). Should she take the horse? No, too old and too slow, she estimated. She could probably make her way more quietly and efficiently on foot. But looking at the horse made her notice the cart. The barrels from the back had been unloaded. Why would her abductors have done that, unless the barrels had been hiding something, just as the straw in the wagon had hidden her? She glanced around to see what the men had concealed beneath the barrels, only to unload here. There it was: a little rowboat on the river's bank, waiting for morning light when the men could set it to water and paddle toward Bittenhelm.

Amelia took two steps toward the river and found the dog clinging to her skirt, holding her back.

"Let go," she demanded in a whisper.

The dog sat down, still holding the edge of her skirt. To move, she would have to drag him across the grass.

If he was a guard dog working for the men, he would never have released her. Was he expressing his opinion that she should use the path?

"We'll take the river," she explained. She felt silly, justifying herself to a dog, but he seemed to understand because he let go of her skirt, then ran ahead and jumped into the boat.

"Fat lot of help you are," she complained as she shoved the boat over the grass and stones that bordered the river at this spot.

The dog may or may not have looked apologetic.

Once the boat was floating, she managed to climb into it without too much difficulty, though the skirt of her gown was soaked up to her knees. She used the oar to push off from the bank, as though this was a punt rather than a rowboat. But it got the job done. Soon they were in water deep enough that the current carried them downstream.

The dog paced nervously, which put them in danger of capsizing.

"Sit!" Amelia commanded.

The dog sat.

Did he look sulky at her abrupt tone?

Don't be silly, she told herself.

Amelia started rowing. She knew how to row, but it wasn't one of her favorite activities. Still, living in a kingdom that had a river as a border, it would have been negligent *not* to know how to row, or to swim.

The dog looked back and forth, from upriver to down.

"We're going to use the same trick the men did," Amelia explained. Again she felt ridiculous explaining her plan to an animal, no matter how smart it appeared. "Just as they headed back *toward* Pastonia to confound pursuers, so *we* will go the opposite way they'd expect us to flee: away from my father's lands and toward Prince Sheridan's."

The dog looked ready to leap overboard.

Amelia finished quickly. "Except we'll bypass Bittenhelm and stay on the river until we get to Fairhaven, which is ruled by King Humphrey, who is an ally to my father. He'll send word to my parents to let them know what's happened and will see me ... us ... safely home."

The dog had given what almost looked like a nod at the name of King Humphrey of Fairhaven, as though to say he knew the king, or that he approved of Amelia's plan.

Obviously the henbane hadn't cleared out of her system as thoroughly as she'd thought, or she wouldn't be attributing all these human reactions to a dog.

Still, he was a very nice dog. And for whatever noble canine reason, he had helped her escape.

The river meandered around tree-lined bends, so already there was no way for the kidnappers to be able to spot them. Besides, they would be searching in the opposite direction. Amelia didn't need to break her back rowing, because the current would carry them downstream. She set the oars down where she could easily reach them, to adjust the course of the boat as needed.

She dipped her hands into the water and scrubbed the last of the remaining berry mixture—and the dog slobber—off her cheeks.

The dog was yawning. Perhaps, in his own way, he'd had as difficult a night as she'd had. Despite all the henbane-induced sleeping she had done, she was exhausted. It couldn't hurt to rest her eyes for a moment . . .

"Princess Amelia," a voice spoke, calm and gentle. "Don't be alarmed."

Amelia knew how things worked. That warning meant there was something to be alarmed *about*.

Her eyes flew open. She should be in a rowboat with a dog, escaping from Prince Sheridan's men . . .

Yes, to the rowboat, *no*, to the dog.

There was a young man sitting on the bench opposite her.

"What have you done with my dog?" Amelia demanded. The dog wasn't, legally speaking, *hers*, but he had helped her and now she felt responsible. Who was this person? How had he gotten here? Was he one of the kidnappers? He *was*! She'd seen him in the straw wagon. What had he done to the dog? She could still smell the faithful though odiferous creature, so if this young man had thrown him overboard—which seemed the only possible explanation, even if she hadn't heard the splash— it must have been only a moment ago.

But Amelia could see no sign of the dog bobbing in the water.

Still speaking in that infuriatingly let's-all-be-calm voice, the intruder said, "I'm Prince Telmund of Rosenmark, and I'm under a spell that transforms me—"

"Transforms?" As an explanation of *anything*, this was the most preposterous lie she'd ever heard.

Amelia picked up one of the oars and smacked the dog-endangering liar on the arm.

"Ouch!" he cried. For a ruffian, he was decidedly not as robust as he should have been. And he was inept. He lunged to prevent her from hitting him again, tipping the boat precariously. He was as unwise about the way a boat worked as the dog had been.

Amelia took advantage of his being off balance and she used her foot to sweep him off his feet. Into the water.

"Help!" he sputtered as he bobbed momentarily to the surface. "I can't swim!"

"A likely story!" she jeered. "This same river runs through Rosenmark! If you really came from there, you'd know how to swim!"

He went under again, and came up hacking and slapping ineffectively at the water.

So maybe *that* part of his story was true. "Well, not learning how to swim was very shortsighted of you," she told him.

But he really was in trouble; she could tell by his panicked flailing.

"Oh for goodness' sake." She extended the oar for him to grab hold of, but he was so frantic he couldn't see it. Or maybe he thought she meant to hit him again.

Amelia couldn't just let him drown.

"Porridge for brains," she mumbled. And she wasn't sure whether she meant him or herself.

She jumped in the water and tried to catch hold of him, but he was coughing and thrashing and kept slipping underwater. By the time she did get her arm hooked around his neck, the rowboat had continued too far downstream to catch, so she dragged him, swimming with only one arm, to the nearer bank.

By then, he was limp and not breathing.

Amelia sat on his back and pounded until the unlikely henchman coughed up several mouthfuls of river water.

"There!" she said. "Now you'd better explain—"

But even as the words were passing her lips, she was sliding off his back, which was growing taller, wider, and rounder. There was no other word for it: He was transforming.

Chapter 9

On the River's Bank

TELMUND

Telmund was pleasantly surprised to find that he was alive. Not only that, but he was on solid ground. Both of these were good things, even if the princess was hitting him, beating on his back. He decided to give her the benefit of the doubt and assume she was trying to knock air into him after nearly killing him by drowning.

Still, this was *not* the way rescued princesses in stories generally acted.

"I'm all right now," he said.

Except it didn't come out that way.

It came out as a bark.

How did that happen?

True, he'd been a dog, but that had stopped when he'd fallen asleep in the rowboat and awakened as himself.

Which, he supposed, could be disconcerting to a delicate princess, so maybe he should have been better prepared for a startled reaction from her.

Not that Amelia *was* delicate, he had to admit. Telmund remembered seeing her dive into the water to rescue him. Nor had he been much use in helping her accomplish this, he grudgingly acknowledged: He may well have hit her with all his arm-waving and floundering, although he'd been too busy screaming for help to be sure. This was not traditional behavior for a story hero. And yet she'd still managed to pull him to shore.

He had no memory of that part of the adventure.

But then he should have turned into *another* animal, not gone backward into being an animal he'd already been.

Was he a different *type* of dog?

Princess Amelia was looking at him with a horrified expression, but that could be because of the transformation itself. Or because he was a big, fierce mastiff. Or maybe a wolf. It might be nice to be a wolf. Did wolves bark?

"Am I a wolf?" he asked. It came out as a strange hollow bark that was not reassuring.

He stretched his paws in front of him to get a look.

Apparently he was a breed of short-legged dog, for he couldn't see anything.

He stretched more, and a startled bark escaped from deep in his chest.

He was an injured dog. Or a malformed one. Or ... or ...

What was wrong with his paws? They didn't even look like paws. They were not individualized into toes. He could push his body up onto them—and it was a massive body, he could tell—but walking was very slow and cumbersome. His back legs were doing little more than dragging.

He looked backward along the length of his sleek, fat body. His back legs were as misshapen as his front. They looked less like a dog's paws than the fins of a big fish, like a sturgeon.

Princess Amelia, who had instinctively backed away from him, now knelt beside him and rested her hand on his head. "Don't be afraid," she said.

That was a fine thing: a princess telling a prince not to be afraid.

Except, of course, he was afraid.

"You're a seal," she told him. "I've seen drawings. There's nothing wrong with you."

How could she tell that was what was terrifying him?

He was reassured, even though he'd never heard of a seal, except for the kind of seal placed on official documents. What was the matter with that witch, turning him into a creature he had never heard of?

"They mostly live on the coast," Amelia told him. "But they can be by lakes, too. They live in the water and on the land. I'm told they're quite graceful in the water."

She didn't have to add, *But not so much on the land.* Telmund had already experienced that.

"I think you'll feel better in the water," she said.

He held up his front leg for her to see how ineffective it was for getting *to* the water.

"That's a flipper," she said. "Dolphins and whales have them, too."

Flipper? Flapper would have been more descriptive, as his limbs flapped pointlessly. And where had Princess Amelia learned this obscure information about all these exotic animals, anyway? She must spend all her time with her nose in exactly the kind of books he avoided: the fact-filled kind that were supposed to teach you something.

Telmund used his flippers to ease himself into the water.

She was right: He was immediately more at ease. He darted back and forth in the comfortable river water, up and down, shallow and deep. He even swam in a circle.

"Very good," Amelia encouraged him.

But it wasn't very good. For one thing, being changed into this bizarre creature opened up all sorts of awful possibilities. What if he *hadn't* been close to the water when he'd become this seal-thing? What if he changed into a *fish* when there wasn't water? Was the witch out to kill him, or was she simply careless?

Also, it wasn't good if he could travel only by water. He didn't have a real sense of where King Humphrey's land of Fairhaven was, having only visited it once, when he'd been much younger. There was a moat, but he knew he didn't remember a river anywhere near the castle.

He waddled to the shallows closest to the princess, looking first in one direction, then the other.

"You're right," Amelia told him. "We would have been leaving the river soon and heading inland. We're close to the southern border of Bittenhelm, and we need to go east for Fairhaven."

It wasn't *exactly* what he'd been wondering, but close enough. Telmund heaved himself out of the water and felt the full weight of his clumsy body.

"No," Amelia said. "You can't travel overland."

He barked at her and proved she was wrong by dragging himself three times the length of his body. Then, exhausted, he had to lie down and rest.

Amelia sat down next to him. "This is the easy part, right by the riverbank, where the ground is smooth. How far do you think you'd get in the forest with all the roots and uneven terrain, and the sharp rocks and twigs?"

Telmund looked at the trees that grew very close together.

"You'd hurt yourself, and you couldn't travel far in any case. Better for us to wait until you change again. You *will* change again, won't you?"

Telmund bobbed his head and barked.

Amelia winced at the piercing sound. "Do you know how long it will be?"

Telmund closed his eyes and rested his head on his flippers, but Amelia guessed wrong about what he was trying to say.

"Yes," she said. "Rest. I'll stay here with you. That will give my clothing a chance to dry."

Telmund shook his head and barked again, even though he knew the sound hurt her ears. It was too dangerous for her to linger with him—even if the thought of being alone and having to find her once again was disheartening.

"You've been tracking me for a while, haven't you?" she asked. She tapped the side of her nose. "I've smelled you here and there. You've been trying to rescue me, haven't you? While I've been totally unmindful of your efforts and even hindering them."

He couldn't argue with her about that.

She smiled, and she had a very nice smile for such a bossy princess. "At least our little swim washed off whatever it was that you'd gotten into, so that's a good thing. And *I* smell better for my bath, too." She nodded, having made up her mind. "I'll stay," she repeated firmly, "now that *you* need help. I'm indebted to you. You rest."

Resting was exactly what he needed. The question was: Should he stay on the land, which was hard and lumpy and seemed to drag down his body? Or should he go back to the water and swim and swim and swim until he wore himself out with exertion?

He waddled back into the water.

Upstream and down, he swam, and from one bank to the other, though never far enough to have her out of his sight. He caught several fish, which he ate raw, and he even tossed one over for the princess, thinking she must be hungry, too. The fish hit her on the back of the head as she was looking around, which she frequently did, clearly on the watch for pursuit. Maybe she didn't know she was meant to eat it, or maybe she preferred her fish cooked. At home, that was the way he'd always had it, but once he got back, he would encourage the kitchen staff to try serving it raw. For now, Amelia flung the fish back at him, looking annoyed.

Telmund was just thinking that the time might be right to lie on the mud by the river's edge and let the sun—which was almost directly overhead—warm his bones and make him grow sleepy.

But just as he started toward the bank, Amelia stood up. "Stay," she commanded unceremoniously in a fierce whisper. "Don't show yourself."

Before he could take offense, Telmund heard what Amelia had clearly heard before him: men talking and laughing, approaching through the woods.

Amelia ran down a length of the bank, then up into the tree line, clearly intent on hiding till she could determine whether the approaching party were the kind of people to be trusted.

Following her don't-show-yourself instruction, Telmund dove low into the water, then bobbed up again to the surface with just enough of his head peeking out that he could see.

It was a hunting party that came out from among the trees: four men, with horses and falcons.

Though Telmund hadn't seen King Humphrey in ages, this man in the expensive and finely cut clothes was clearly not him. But, just as clearly, he was royalty. That left—assuming Princess Amelia's geography wasn't at fault—Prince Sheridan.

This impression was strengthened by the way the man talked, complaining bitterly that one of his companions had gotten the party lost and that he would be beaten soundly once they got back.

"But see, my lord, here is the river. We're almost within hailing distance of the southernmost hunting lodge." The man pointed in the direction that lodge must be. "We can water the horses here, spend the night at the camp, then head off to the castle tomorrow morning."

"I wanted to be there this afternoon, you incompetent fool. Stop talking, or I may decide to press your family into servitude to make up for your blunder."

One of the other men dismounted and examined the mud on the riverbank while the horses drank.

Prince Sheridan said, "If you're going to tell me the stag passed this way, so I should show mercy to this dolt, don't even think about it."

"Not a deer," the man said. "A person. Someone with small, delicate feet. A woman, by my estimation." The man started following the footsteps in the direction Amelia had gone.

What should I do? Telmund thought frantically. Should he call out—well, he couldn't call out, but should he bark out—a warning to Amelia to run? But maybe it was better not to. Maybe the man couldn't make sense of the jumble of foot- and flipper/flapper-prints, and wouldn't be able to track her *unless* she broke cover and ran.

Stay where you are, Telmund mentally urged her. *You'd never be able to outrun them. Maybe he won't see you.*

Telmund heard the snap of a twig. She must have decided there was no way the hunter *couldn't* find her. A moment later she was running into the woods.

The man ran after her.

Still hiding in the water, Telmund could hear the scuffle. It was short-lived. The man came back into view, holding Princess Amelia under his arm as though she were a sack of onions. Amelia kicked and slapped at his arms and legs, and used words most princesses would not.

Telmund swam closer to the shore. But what could he do? There was no way he could surprise the men, not if he had to travel on the ground. And once they saw him . . . Well, they were hunters. Whether they knew about seals, he was still a big catch. A big, lumbering, good-for-nothing catch. He paddled back out to the center of the river.

Prince Sheridan was laughing at the antics of Princess Amelia trying to escape her captor. But then, suddenly, he realized who she was.

"Can it be?" he crowed. "I sent three of my men to fetch you and bring you to my castle this afternoon, and just as I learn I will miss that appointment, here you come looking for me!"

He got off his horse and approached, which Telmund had to admit was taking a risk, what with her arms and legs flailing.

Prince Sheridan snatched her hand and kissed it. "Well met, my prize, my bride-to-be!"

"Never!" Amelia shouted at him.

Prince Sheridan laughed. "We'll see."

AMELIA

"Stay!" Amelia commanded the seal who was really a prince, lest he try something foolhardy and get himself captured or killed.

Well, that was presumptuous of me, she thought a moment later, *assuming that he'd endanger himself for my sake.* Still, he'd been following her as a rabbit and a dog and a person for a couple days now, and even if that wasn't putting himself in danger, it certainly had to be an inconvenience.

Meanwhile, Prince Sheridan was looking puzzled and, truth be told, a bit put out. With no one in sight that she could have been addressing, he had to suppose she was taking that tone with him.

To take attention away from the fact that his just-proclaimed bride-to-be may well have addressed him as though he were a disobedient lapdog, he turned away and remounted his horse. But then he asked his men, "Is there any sign of anyone else about?"

The two men who weren't holding on to her dismounted to examine the riverbank.

They conferred about the marks in the mud.

"Well?" Prince Sheridan demanded impatiently.

"No sign of another person," one of the men said. "Some creature appears to have come onshore then returned to the water. Perhaps an enormous turtle . . . ?"

Hesitantly, the other said, "Or maybe a really fat otter?"

It was obvious neither of the men knew anything or even believed what they themselves were suggesting. They were just taking wild guesses.

With a dismissive shrug, Prince Sheridan declared, "If it came from the water and returned to the water, it's of no interest to us." Apparently he didn't have an inquiring mind, and that was one more reason to dislike him.

Another reason was the way he patted his thigh in a gesture Amelia associated with her father beckoning one of his hounds to sit by him.

The man who'd caught Amelia hoisted her up in front of the prince. Sitting astride would be unladylike, of course, so he placed her with her right side to the prince, rather than her back. It was uncomfortable, as well as precarious. But Amelia would *not* put her arm around him to make her seating more secure.

Prince Sheridan took hold of her by the hair, not exactly yanking, but not gently, either, and pulled her head back. "We're not going to try anything foolish, are we, my dear?" he asked.

She was frightened, but even more than that, she was angry. Still, neither reaction would help her now. What she had to be was brave. And smart.

She could bide her time. Telmund would have heard where Prince Sheridan was taking her—toward his southernmost hunting lodge. Once Telmund turned back into a person, he could either follow the river back to her home to tell her father what had happened, or he could continue on to Fairhaven and enlist the help of their ally, King Humphrey.

Assuming Telmund didn't get lost on the way. Given the ease with which she'd been able to shove him out of both straw wagon and boat—not to mention that he was a prince whose family's castle was on an island and yet he had never learned how to swim—Amelia didn't have much confidence in his abilities.

He's young, she reminded herself. Still, she suspected that even a year or two ago, when she'd been his age, she'd had more common sense.

For now the prudent thing for her to do was not to enrage Prince Sheridan.

"Nothing foolish," she assured him from between clenched teeth.

He gave her a light kiss on the throat as though to seal the bargain.

She knew that—in the way of marriages arranged for diplomacy and alliances—there often was a big difference in the age between the partners. That knowledge didn't help. Prince Sheridan was her parents' age, and his intentionally menacing yet flirtatious manner was unsettling. She rubbed her wrist over the spot as though she could wipe the kiss away.

He laughed and dug his heels into his horse's sides with a suddenness that caused the animal to lurch forward and Amelia to fall sideways into his arms. His men scurried to mount their horses, lest they get left behind.

A moment later, as they rode into the woods, the prince complained, "You're damp."

"I was swimming with the mysterious creature from the river," she said.

The prince snorted.

"You better not have let anything come out of your nose and onto my hair with that snort," Amelia scolded, going for an I-am-a-princess-so-I-can-say-whatever-thought-crosses-my-mind tone.

"What?" the prince asked. "No." He pouted, though he probably would have called it a glower. "You say strange things."

"Stranger than: 'Ooo, I think I want to marry this princess I've never met before, even if it means sending some dim-witted ruffians to kidnap her, putting her very life in danger'?"

"I never actually used those exact words," Prince Sheridan informed her. "What I said was: Bring her to me—however you can."

Evidently, he was trying to be on good behavior for the princess he planned to marry. Good. She could probably get away with a certain amount of needling.

"Close enough," Amelia snapped, ready to be a thorn in his side.

Prince Sheridan shrugged. "Don't whine," he said.

Whine? WHINE? He had the nerve to think she was whining?

Amelia took a deep breath. "So, why so eager to marry me? Have you heard tales of my great beauty and sophistication? My sense of style? How well I dance? What great company I am, and how likely I am to be meek and deferential and give in to my husband's wishes?"

If he had troubled himself to learn anything about her, she knew those would not be the things he'd heard. And she could only imagine that by now she looked even less princesslike than she had to the henchmen who'd been so unimpressed with her appearance. Amelia had been without the ministrations of her maid, Constance, for two days now. She'd slept first in a wagon hauling straw, then on the ground, then in a rowboat, and *then* she'd jumped into the river to rescue the young sometimes-an-animal-sometimes-a-human prince.

As for Telmund, she was beginning to think more highly of *him* ever since starting this conversation with Prince Sheridan.

Once again, Prince Sheridan snorted. He ignored the way Amelia reached back and ran her hand over her hair as though to check nothing had gotten on it.

He said, "It's nothing to do with you personally, and everything to do with politics."

"Ah!" Amelia said as though this explained all. "You need a likable wife so that your own people will give up their plans to rise up in rebellion against you."

"What?" demanded Prince Sheridan. "My people aren't plotting rebellion."

"Oops." Amelia placed a hand over her mouth, as though she'd committed a faux pas. "Well, if we're lucky, maybe the rumors aren't true."

"What rumors?" Prince Sheridan demanded. "What have you heard?"

"Nothing," Amelia answered in all truth, knowing that her tone and his suspicious mind would make him believe she was simply refusing to say.

He tightened his grip on the reins. "I can easily quash any rebellion," he told her.

"That's the spirit!" she declared encouragingly. "Think positive thoughts! Meanwhile—given that there is obviously no rebellion planned in your realm or you would have heard about it—please explain to me what you meant about our marriage having to do with politics."

Prince Sheridan hesitated, perhaps trying to sort through what might have been concealed in her words. "Your father is allied with King Humphrey of Fairhaven."

At the mention of her father, Amelia felt her heart was likely to break from missing her parents—from worrying about them worrying about her. She wanted to slap Prince Sheridan for daring to hurt them so.

Be brave, she reminded herself, *but smart, too.*

Prince Sheridan didn't react to her silence. Perhaps he thought she was too foolish and frivolous to concern herself with matters of politics and alliances. He explained, "I want King Humphrey's lands."

Of course he did, the greedy man!

"And he doesn't have a daughter?" Amelia knew very well that he did. Princess Gabriella of Fairhaven was older than Amelia, so they weren't exactly friends. But Amelia knew Gabriella was happily married to someone from the fairy realm.

And Prince Sheridan knew this, too. "She's already married," he said dismissively. "Her father didn't choose wisely in permitting an alliance with someone who brought no lands or prestige with him."

As if King Humphrey would ever have consented to let his daughter marry a villain like Prince Sheridan!

"There's only so much," she murmured as though agreeing, "that can be said for mutual love and respect."

Prince Sheridan obviously thought she was too silly to be able to put such matters together. "If I marry you, then your father won't dare oppose me when I march on Fairhaven. He'll have your safety to consider. Then, when my father dies, as he must sooner or later, and your father dies with you as his only heir, I'll have control of three kingdoms. That's worth more than mutual love and respect any day."

"You're very good at plotting things out," Amelia said. "A little slow to come to your conclusions, but I suppose it's the getting there that's important, not how long the journey takes."

"You dare to speak to me so impudently?" Prince Sheridan demanded, so angrily that Amelia worried she might have pushed too far.

"I only meant that if you had come up with this plan ten years or so ago, you could have married Princess Gabriella rather than me, then overrun *our* kingdom without worry of reprisal from King Humphrey." Amelia lowered her voice conspiratorially, though none of the prince's men rode anywhere close enough to overhear. "I *do* understand that she is lovely and, generally speaking, the epitome of what a princess should be. There's no doubt that your unsettled masses would have fallen in love with her and there'd be none of this talk of rebellion."

"There *is* no talk of rebellion," Prince Sheridan insisted. "No one would dare risk my wrath!"

Amelia turned to give him a wink. "We'll say no more about it," she told him. "I'm just saying: If you had been smart e—" She cut herself off as though this had been a slip of the tongue. She started again more slowly. "If you had been cunning enough . . . No, wait. If you'd seen the opportunity ten years ago—"

"You talk too much," Prince Sheridan said.

"I'm usually not accused of that," Amelia said. "I'm just saying: If you need help thinking things out—"

"I do not need help thinking things out!"

As annoying as she was being, Amelia trusted that Prince Sheridan wouldn't let her fall off the horse—certainly not with people watching. She extended both hands out, palms up, as though weighing two stones. "I'm just saying: Me. Princess Gabriella. Me. Princess Gabriella. M—"

"Stop talking!" the prince commanded.

"Just trying to help."

"I don't need help," Prince Sheridan said. "I couldn't marry Princess Gabriella when she was available because . . ." He cut himself off.

Amelia smirked. "You'll think of some excuse eventually."

"I'm not trying to think of an excuse. It's just none of your business."

"Good one!" Amelia cheered. "Ooo, I've got another one you can use in these situations: *You wouldn't understand.* Isn't that a good one, too? Or how about this? *I WOULD tell you, but it's in the best interests of the country that I don't.* I think that's an excellent one. Versatile, too. Depending on the circumstances, you could change it to *the best interests of the family.* Or . . ." She gestured expansively to include the prince's men. "*The hunting party.* Or *the welfare of the world as we know it.* Or—"

"Stop," Prince Sheridan commanded, "talking."

"Or, yes," Amelia told him sweetly, "you can just use the power of your I-am-the-prince-and-you-must-do-my-bidding voice. Nobody will accuse you of being as witless as a slug and incapable of coming up with a rebuttal. So just leave it at that."

She deepened her voice to sound more commanding. *"I couldn't marry Princess Gabriella because I am the prince, and I didn't want to."*

Clearly, Prince Sheridan didn't want anyone—even a princess who wouldn't stop talking—thinking of him as witless. "I needed time to get out of a betrothal my father had made for me."

"Really?" That was a surprise. "With whom?"

"Never mind."

"Didn't you love her?"

"I never met her."

"Then why did you *not* want to marry her?"

"Because I knew I could do better."

Amelia considered. Not that she'd wish Prince Sheridan onto anyone, but to break a betrothal was serious business, and he was lucky the aggrieved father hadn't declared war. "That wasn't nice," she said.

Smugly, Prince Sheridan said, "But it *was* smart."

That just about said it all.

"So who was she?" Amelia asked.

Prince Sheridan shook his head.

"Why won't you tell me?"

"You wouldn't know her."

"I know a lot of people."

"You wouldn't know *her.*"

"My parents like to give balls, and I've met—"

The prince pulled up on his horse's reins. "Galt," he called over his shoulder.

One of the men drew closer. "My lord?"

"Would you take this damp and annoying princess off my hands?"

The man held his arm out to take Amelia over onto his horse.

Amelia left him waiting while she tapped her finger to her lips conspiratorially and said to Prince Sheridan, "My lips are sealed. I won't tell this man anything about the rebellion."

"There *is* no rebellion!"

"Good gracious! Certainly not!" Amelia let herself be transferred to the other horse and didn't speak a word to the man Galt all the rest of the way to the hunting lodge.

~ *Chapter 10* ~

The Hunting Lodge

TELMUND

Amelia had told him to stay, and really, there was nothing else Telmund could do.

But, on the other hand (or rather, on the other flipper), *How can I possibly just lie down and go to sleep when the exact thing I've been trying to prevent has happened?* Telmund asked himself. There were no stories Telmund had ever heard that said, "Watching the villain carrying the princess off, the hero settled himself down for a nap."

But no story he had ever heard had the hero changing from one creature to another in between naps, either. He was useless to Amelia as a seal and needed to hasten his transformation into a person.

After Prince Sheridan and his men left, Telmund crawled out of the water and onto the riverbank.

It was late afternoon, but the sun was still warm and Telmund worked hard at emptying his mind rather than letting it swim around in circles. He gave himself up to enjoying the sensation of the sun evaporating the water from his furry skin and wouldn't allow words to bubble up into his brain—especially ones like *useless* and *coward* and *shameful*. He only thought of images: the sun in the sky, the sparkles on the water, the fish darting close by. (Because, even if you aren't currently hungry, it's nice to know there's a ready supply of food swimming around waiting for you.)

The rest of him had dried in the sun, but Telmund woke up with one foot in the water.

At least it was a foot and no longer one of those flipper/ flapper things.

And at least the sun, though alarmingly low in the sky, was still shining bright enough to see by, though nighttime's shadows would be closing in shortly.

He had seen which way the men had taken the princess, and he hoped the one man had been accurate when he'd indicated Prince Sheridan's hunting lodge was nearby.

Ignoring the unpleasant squishy sensation of his right foot in his soaked boot (physical discomfort meant nothing to story heroes, who could continue despite grievous wounds), Telmund headed off into the woods. It was darker among the trees, but the horses' passage had broken through the underbrush, and he was able to follow that trail until—not too very much farther along—he came to an actual path. He examined both directions until he found hoofprints leading off to the left. This was something that the hero of an adventure story would have done, and Telmund felt a pride and satisfaction that he was finally accomplishing something. Hopefully, the path led directly to the hunting lodge without any branching off, because by now it was too dark to make out any details beyond *clear path* and *wall of bordering trees*. And even that wasn't always as apparent as it could have been.

And then, happy sign, he could smell smoke from a wood fire, and he was able to follow his nose the remainder of his way to the lodge.

His own father had two hunting lodges, both big enough to accommodate substantial hunting parties, including houndsmen, falconers, servants, and cooks. Prince Sheridan's lodge was bigger than either of those in Rosenmark.

Prince Sheridan's lodge was bigger than *both* the lodges in Rosenmark put together.

There were three outbuildings. One was the kitchen, separate so as to minimize the likelihood of a cook fire spreading to the main building; one was to house the horses; one was for the falcons—falcons being notoriously easy to startle and injure themselves. The stable and mews were dark. The kitchen and main building both had windows whose shutters were open to let in the cool evening breeze, and light poured out into the darkness from several of these.

Telmund peeked first into the back window of the kitchen, which was the least likely to tell him anything but a good one on which to practice, since that was the one where he was least likely to be noticed. A story hero might not need practice spying, but it was more important to recognize his limitations than to just jump into things without thinking. He hoped he

135

could be one of those heroes who succeeded by relying on his wits rather than on physical ability, because he had to acknowledge that fighting and swordplay were not his strengths.

Even ignoring his squishy boot was not one of his strengths. A story hero should not be telling himself he hoped he wouldn't develop a blister.

In the kitchen, a cook and her two assistants tended the cook fires in the hearths. They stirred, ladled, carved, dusted with flour, and did other kitcheny things. A procession of serving boys took the platters and carried them out the door and into the main building. The only one not moving at a frantic pace was a scullery maid who sat hunched in the corner close to one of the fires. The rest of the staff was probably being lenient with her because she would be up long after everyone else had gone to bed, cleaning up spills, scouring dishes and pots, banking all the fires, preparing everything to start all over again in the morning.

Telmund ran to the lodge itself in a low crouch to lessen the chances of being seen. Still, once he reached the building, he had to stand on tiptoe and hold on to the window ledge before he could see into the main hall.

Many people were present, but no Princess Amelia.

He had hoped the hunting party of four would be all the men he had to worry about.

Instead, Prince Sheridan and about two dozen of his men sat at tables, while the kitchen boys brought in a steady supply of more food, and serving girls kept plates and goblets full. A minstrel played a lute and tried to keep the men entertained, but apparently Prince Sheridan didn't think he was doing a satisfactory job. Just as Telmund looked into the window, the prince flung a half loaf of bread at the musician. A variety of other foodstuffs already littered the floor around the man: a gnawed-on drumstick, an artichoke, a head of cabbage, a goblet that had not been empty when it was thrown.

Or maybe *the throwing* was the entertainment.

There was much loud talk and rowdy laughter and boisterous flirting with the serving girls. Telmund thought some of the laughter sounded forced, to keep the prince in good cheer, but that might have been only because *he* did not find the prince as humorous as the prince seemed to find himself.

This was not gentle company for a gentle princess, and Telmund was relieved that Princess Amelia was not present to be subjected to this.

Not, he had to admit to himself, that she was exactly a gentle princess.

More importantly, if she wasn't here, where was she?

Maybe she had retired to a bedchamber already?

Stealthily, Telmund walked around the building, trying to see into each window, but some of the shutters were closed. He considered tapping—but what if a room was occupied by someone other than Amelia?

His second circuit around the building, he listened with his ear pressed to the fastened shutters. He could hear two servants talking in one room, which probably meant that Amelia wasn't there. Some very unfeminine snoring came from another room, and some indistinct stirring in another—which might have been

137

a servant making up a bed, or someone (a princess?) tossing and turning in agitation. Other rooms were totally quiet, which might mean they were empty, or might mean someone inside was simply totally quiet.

On one whole side of the building, Telmund had to be on the alert and ready to duck down or flatten himself against a wall so as to avoid being seen by the near-continual succession of kitchen boys replenishing the food for the table.

Did people eat that much in his father's castle?

He decided to take another look into the kitchen, to calculate how much longer the meal might last.

There was still basting and turning of a guinea fowl on a spit, as well as hard-boiled egg peeling, bottle uncorkings, and scraping of used dishes. The scullery maid still hadn't bestirred herself, and that was going to get her in trouble probably sooner rather than later, as the two assistants were beginning to get anxious and shrill with each other. Telmund had just registered that he wasn't seeing the cook when a door he hadn't even been aware of banged open and the cook—holding a bucket of water to be dumped—stepped out right next to where he was standing.

"What are you doing back here?" she demanded.

Story heroes are always quick thinkers and glib with making up believable and diverting excuses.

Telmund said, "Ahmmm ..."

"Did you get lost between the lodge and here?" The question was spoken in pointed jest, as the distance was less than a hundred yards, with a clear line of sight.

Telmund said, "Ahmmm . . ."

The cook sighed. "You one of the new boys the steward hired on?"

Telmund nodded energetically.

"Not very big in the brains category, are you?"

Telmund said, "Ahmmm . . ."

The cook emptied the water onto the grass, then handed him the bucket. "Smart enough to fill this?"

Telmund was about to say *Ahmmm . . .* , but the cook took him by the shoulders, turned him around so that he was facing the well, and gave him a little shove, maybe to encourage him, or maybe she had so little confidence in him she wanted to make sure he started off in the right direction.

Filling a bucket might be the work of a servant, not a hero, but Telmund did as he'd been told. Without too much difficulty.

By the time he was finished, the cook had gone back into the kitchen, so Telmund followed her inside, where he found her busy beating some eggs to a froth in a bowl.

He cleared his throat, but nobody looked up.

The two assistants had stopped their bickering and were adding logs to one of the fires, which was really a scullery maid's duty. The scullery maid, Telmund could see from this new angle, was not really hunched over but was crouched beside a cat. She was, in fact, talking earnestly to the cat. The cat was cleaning its paw.

Telmund took a closer look. Despite the servant-girl clothing, and even though her hair hung straight and scraggly, having been wet in the river, then never combed out, once Telmund could see her face, he recognized Princess Amelia.

He asked, louder than he needed to in order to get Amelia's attention off the cat, "Where should I put this bucket?"

"On the counter," the cook said without looking up.

But the important thing was that Princess Amelia looked up. Then she looked at the cat. Then she looked at Telmund again. Then she looked at the cat, who yawned and curled up to sleep. Amelia sighed.

She stood and took a step toward him, but Telmund held his hand up in warning for her to stay.

Telmund put the bucket down, then announced, "The prince said to fetch . . . her." Had Prince Sheridan informed the kitchen staff who the girl he'd left with them really was? He must have, otherwise they'd have set her to work. But then why was she dressed like a maid?

The cook set aside the bowl with the eggs and looked at Amelia. "Are your clothes dried yet, honey?" she asked.

Telmund finally noticed the pile of what-had-once-been finery that was placed close to the fire's warmth.

Amelia prodded it. "Yes," she said. "Thank you."

"Take 'em into the pantry and change there," the cook instructed. "Can you get dressed by yourself?"

"Why wouldn't I?" Amelia asked.

The cook shrugged. "Some of the fine ladies who come need their maids. But they bring their own. As well as proper gowns in case they tire of one or need to change. There's some up at the castle as could help you, but here you'd have to settle for Ita."

The assistant who must have been Ita started to wipe her hands on her apron.

"I'm fine," Amelia assured them. "I'll only be a moment."

"And you," the cook said to Telmund as Amelia stepped into the privacy of the pantry, "you tell His Royal Highness that's no way to treat a princess, setting her down in the kitchen to dry just because he thought the day was too warm to put in a fire at the big house. You tell him princesses are delicate."

Telmund nodded, though he was becoming less and less convinced about how delicate Amelia was.

The cook sighed. "Never mind," she grumbled. "You'd only get in trouble for speaking out."

Telmund nodded again.

The cook sighed—this time at him, not the injustice of the world—and returned to her work.

It took Amelia more than a few moments, during which time other serving boys came and went, but when Amelia stepped out of the pantry, she looked more like her old self.

"God go with you, honey," the cook told her.

"Thank you," Amelia said, "for all your kindness."

Then she and Telmund stepped out into the night.

"I thought the cat was you," Amelia whispered to him.

"Ahm . . ." Telmund whispered back. "No, it wasn't."

Mentally, he kicked himself for being a lackwit. *Glib*, he reminded himself. *Diverting*.

Amelia tipped her face up to the sky.

Telmund wondered if she was savoring her freedom, or checking to see if it was likely to rain. He glanced up and saw stars twinkling in a cloudless dark blue.

She must be savoring her freedom, because she was still looking.

Continuing to speak in a hushed tone, he warned, "We should get moving."

She followed him to the edge of the clearing on which the lodge was built before she asked, "Where are we going?"

"Uhm," Telmund said, "away from Prince Sheridan."

"Short term, yes," Amelia said. "Long term?"

Who talked like that? "I thought you said we should go to Fairhaven, to seek help from King Humphrey."

"That was while we were by the river. I'm not sure I could find my way there from deep within these woods—at least, not at night. You?"

Telmund suspected she was not being sarcastic but was really asking. "No," he admitted.

"Did you leave markers on the trail to be able to make our way back to where we left the river?"

And that was something Telmund recognized that many a hero of a story was likely to do.

He shook his head, which she might or might not have been able to see in the dark. If not, she took his silence correctly.

"Well," she said, "I do think that I can get us back to Pastonia from here."

"From here?" he repeated doubtfully.

"Yes," she said. "By the stars. I noted them as we left the lodge."

Oh. That was what she'd been doing, looking up at the sky—not daydreaming. He knew seafarers used the stars, but he wasn't sure exactly how.

Before his brother Frederic had left home to get married and be ambassador to the fairy court, he used to point out the constellations to Telmund. There were stories to go with some of the stars, and Telmund liked the stories. He just wasn't very good at recognizing the patterns in the night sky. When Frederic traced the outlines with his finger, the pictures were there. Otherwise, not.

Now, even though the trees under which they stood hid the sky, Amelia pointed up past them to where she had seen some star she had recognized. "That's where the polestar is, due north. So that means east, for Pastonia, would be . . ." She pointed which direction they should go.

"Yes," Telmund conceded, "fine. But we won't be able to see the stars to keep our bearings once we're surrounded by the trees." "Keeping one's bearings" was a phrase he'd heard in a nautical story.

Amelia said, "True, but so long as the terrain doesn't force us in directions we don't want to go, and so long as Prince Sheridan and his men don't come after us, we should be back home before nightfall tomorrow."

Did this princess know everything there was to know about every subject in the world? Telmund was simultaneously relieved, annoyed, impressed, and humiliated. "Those are two big *so long as*'s," he said grumpily.

Amelia glanced back over her shoulder.

Telmund looked also—to make sure there was no one there.

They could still see the lodge, its windows looking bright and merry. But no sign—not yet—of pursuit.

AMELIA

For a long time Amelia and Telmund walked in silence, just in case Prince Sheridan really did send to the kitchen for her and her absence was noted.

Also, the going was rough. The trees' branches only occasionally let moonlight through, so a certain amount of concentration was needed to keep from falling or walking into something—including each other.

Amelia found it exhilarating—though somewhat unnerving—to be putting to use lessons she'd learned while studying in the comfort of home and family. She'd always known these skills were important, vital even, but this was different. Having the responsibility of her and Telmund's safety out in the real world, without any tutors to fall back on, without any books to be able to check her facts, without anyone to encourage her that she was on the right track—this was wearing. Her parents must feel this strain all the time, being responsible for an entire kingdom.

But after a while, Amelia couldn't take the silence any longer—not when she had so many questions that needed answering. "Tell me about the spell that turns you into different creatures," she said. "Who put it on you?"

"A witch," Telmund muttered.

Amelia suspected witches were mostly used in stories in order to encourage misbehaving children to behave. "Often," she informed Telmund, "those who get accused of being witches are only eccentric or unlikable women."

144

"Well, then," Telmund said by way of correction, "if not a witch, then an eccentric and unlikable woman with magical powers."

It was no use arguing. Clearly, *someone* had put a spell on the young man.

"But why?" Amelia asked.

Telmund sighed. "It was the whole youngest-brother predicament."

Amelia considered. "Witches don't like youngest brothers?" she asked.

Even in the darkness, she could tell the look Telmund turned on her was startled. "On the contrary; they prefer youngest brothers."

Amelia didn't bother to ask *why*. She only observed, "Which you are not." She knew from her studies of the nearby kingdoms that King Leopold of Rosenmark had five sons. She didn't remember all their names (Prince Leopold and Prince Baldwin were the oldest two, and the ones she was most likely to encounter or have dealings with), but she recalled that the youngest was *quite* young, under ten years old. So Telmund must be the next youngest. "Still," she said, trying to work it out in her mind, "certainly witches can't go around putting spells on all the people they meet who are *not* youngest sons—else we'd start running out of people."

Telmund stopped walking and just looked at her.

"What?" she asked.

He shook his head but resumed walking. "For all the reading you obviously do . . . ," he started.

"What?" she repeated. In her experience, sentences that started that way generally did not end well. "I'm trying to understand so that we can work this out together."

Telmund said, "Once there was a father who had three sons . . ."

"Yes?" Amelia urged, once it became obvious Telmund planned to leave it at that.

"Sometimes it's daughters. It makes no difference."

"Really?" Amelia asked. "No difference between sons and daughters? Tell that to a parent."

Telmund sighed. "For story purposes it makes no difference. A man, or a woman, has three sons, or three daughters."

"What if there are two sons and one daughter?" Amelia asked. "Or two daughters and one son?"

"No," Telmund told her. "All the same. And the older two are always greedy and cruel and lazy, and the youngest is always generous, clean of heart, and hardworking."

Amelia couldn't just let something that plainly inaccurate pass. "I haven't necessarily found that to be true," she said. "That seems a judgmental and potentially harmful thing to assume. Different families have different experiences, and sometimes the older are spoiled, and sometimes the younger, and sometimes all the offspring, and sometimes none."

"I'm talking about in stories." For some reason, Telmund's voice was beginning to sound frayed.

Even so, Amelia couldn't help saying it: "Stories are a waste of time."

Telmund didn't answer, and after a while, it became obvious he wasn't planning to.

"Aren't you going to finish?" she asked.

"You just said it's a waste of time."

"I said *stories* are a waste of time."

"It's all connected," Telmund told her.

And, irritatingly, he waited for her to come out and actually say, "Go on, then," before he continued.

"So this witch, seeing me with my younger brother, Wilmar, assumed I was a bully and needed to be punished. Or taught a lesson. I'm not quite sure what she was thinking."

"*Were* you bullying Wilmar?" She didn't think that sounded like him, but really, she didn't know him that well.

"No. It was a judgmental and harmful thing she assumed. So she changed me into a rat, and I ended up getting thrown into the river."

Horrified, Amelia said, "That's awful."

"I think so, too," Telmund agreed.

"You can't swim," Amelia said. "Did she know you can't swim? Was she *trying* to drown you?"

"Well, it wasn't her who threw me into the water. And I could swim as a rat. When I'm an animal, I'm both me and the animal, sharing the same body. So, since a rat would know how to swim, *I* knew how to swim. But the river current was strong, and I ended up getting swept downstream until I could finally get out—which turned out to be in Pastonia. Once I woke up from the ordeal, I was a boy again. But the fairy explained to me: Each time I wake up, I'm a different animal. I can't control *which* animal I'm going to turn into, but I'm always a boy in between."

"Wait a moment," Amelia said suspiciously. "You said it was a *witch* who put the spell on you."

"It was."

"So then, where did this fairy come from?"

"Your garden."

"We don't have a fairy in our garden."

"Yes, you do."

"No, we don't."

Telmund sighed and once again fell silent.

"Stop sulking," Amelia said.

"I'm not sulking."

Amelia considered. Eventually, she asked, "So, are witches fairies who have turned bad?"

"I have no idea," Telmund answered. "But I wouldn't think so. Fairies help animals. That's how I met the fairy in your garden: She was willing to help me, but only while I was a rabbit."

Amelia shook her head, figuring they could come back to this, if need be.

Meanwhile, Telmund continued, "She put me in the same wagon those men were using to smuggle you away from your home. That was how I came to learn what was going on."

"Did she mean for you to rescue me, then?" Amelia asked. She was remembering the strange girl the night of the ball. Her being a fairy might explain much.

"I don't know," Telmund admitted. "I think she only meant to get me out of there so she wouldn't have to deal with me. She refused to break the spell."

Amelia asked, "How does one go about breaking a spell?"

"I have no idea about that, either."

Amelia insisted, "Your stories don't tell you that?"

Telmund sighed. Amelia thought he sighed a lot. But she had to acknowledge that maybe this was just her effect on him. Her parents sighed a lot, too. Amelia suddenly wondered if maybe she had that effect on people in general.

"In stories," Telmund explained, "there are different ways to break different spells. But I've never heard of a spell like this one."

Amelia nodded. "But give me an example of one way to break a spell."

"True love's first kiss," Telmund told her.

"Nice try," Amelia said.

She meant it as a joke—after all, there was no reason to think he'd *want* to kiss her—but Telmund made sputtering, choking sounds. "No . . . I didn't mean . . . I . . . You . . ." He gave a very exasperated sigh.

Amelia couldn't tell if the idea of kissing her had embarrassed or appalled him.

In either case, "Still," she said, talking to cover her humiliation, "I don't see the value of stories if they pose problems but don't give solutions."

Once again, Telmund stopped in his tracks. "I wouldn't even be here if it weren't for stories," he said.

Amelia nodded. "Yes, I understand. Because the witch made assumptions based on stories."

"No." Telmund pointed to directly where he stood. "I wouldn't be *here*. I wanted to be like the heroes in the stories, who do brave deeds, who help those in need, who keep trying and never give up, and who are unmindful of what danger they might get into if they do the right thing."

Amelia couldn't let that pass without poking fun at it. Especially after having had her self-assurance battered by his reaction to her comment about not kissing her. She scoffed. "To put yourself in danger to help someone else?"

"*Especially* to help someone else," Telmund said.

His words sucked all the air out of Amelia's lungs. "You've been trying to rescue me because of the stories you've read?"

"Yes," he said.

It was hard to make fun of someone who said something like that.

Chapter 11

Reunion

TELMUND

In those places where the trees grew less densely clustered and permitted limited views of bits of the starry sky, Amelia would take an accounting of where they were and occasionally make minor adjustments to their course.

I will not fall asleep. I will not fall asleep, Telmund kept repeating to himself as he grew weary of all the walking. The last thing they needed was him turning into something else.

Eventually the woods thinned enough that they could see the sky more often than not, but by then they didn't need the stars—which had grown too dim to be sure of anyway—because the sun was just beginning to peek up over the edge of the world.

"Well, at least now we can be certain which direction is east," Telmund said.

"I was certain before," Amelia told him.

"Of course you were," he answered.

She glanced away from him, and he suspected that—had there been enough light—he would have been able to see her blush. He wanted to tell her that he hadn't meant the statement as a criticism. He was only acknowledging her superior abilities.

Of which he was a little envious.

A little more than a little.

But he let the moment pass and didn't tell her.

They had been alert for sounds of anyone else, especially any sounds coming from behind them, the direction from which pursuers sent by Prince Sheridan were most likely to arrive.

So Telmund was taken completely by surprise when he caught a sudden blurred glimpse of someone rushing at him from off to his right.

The *sudden* was because the person had been hiding behind a tree until the last moment; the *blurred* was because of the speed of the person before he actually caught up to Telmund, clapping a hand over his mouth as though to prevent him from calling out; and the *glimpse* was because in another moment Telmund's senses swam—probably something to do with the fact that it wasn't an empty hand held over his mouth but a cloth with a familiar smell.

He still didn't have a name to put to the scent, but his human brain screeched, as clearly as his rabbit brain had in the wagon where the kidnappers were transporting the drugged Princess Amelia: *Not good! Danger!*

And then all thoughts dissolved into nothingness.

AMELIA

Amelia heard a muffled *thump* and turned to see that Prince Sheridan's henchman Willum had come out of seemingly nowhere to seize Telmund.

She had perhaps one moment when she might have been able to elude Jud, who was slightly slower in coming at her from her left. But she recognized what Willum was doing and instead she remained where she was, in order to shout at him: "Enough! Too much henbane and you'll be the death of him!"

By then, Jud had wrapped his arms around her from behind, so escape was no longer a possibility.

Amelia made no move to struggle. She told Willum, "Prince Sheridan will be very angry if you kill him."

Willlum didn't look sure, but he stepped back from Telmund. Without the support, Telmund slipped to the ground.

"Who is he?" Willum asked her.

"Someone who helped me escape from Prince Sheridan." She could say that because it wasn't giving away anything, merely stating the obvious. Amelia didn't volunteer the information that Telmund had also helped her escape from *them*. Seeing Willum look down at Telmund's still body, she hurried to add, "The prince will want to question him. Perhaps he will forgive you the disgrace of having lost me, if you bring both of us back."

Willum looked at the henbane-soaked cloth in his hand, clearly considering whether to use it on her.

"Do you think Prince Sheridan wants me dim-witted and slack-jawed from henbane?" Amelia asked.

"Still, prob'ly safest to do it," Jud told Willum.

"Nobody's talking to you," Willum said.

He thought some more, then finally put the cloth in his pocket.

Amelia tried not to look too relieved.

From another pocket, he withdrew a length of rope, and he crooked his finger for Jud to bring Amelia closer. "I'll tie her this time," he said, "seeing as how you bungled the job last time."

"I did no—" Jud started to protest.

"Nobody's talking to you," Willum repeated, which made no sense at all.

Once Amelia's wrists were bound, he told her, "You walk along beside us now, and don't give us no trouble."

"No trouble from me," Amelia agreed.

Then with Willum at Telmund's feet, and Jud holding on to the sleeping prince by the shoulders, they hoisted the youngster up and carried him, not a great distance, to where their cart and its tired gray horse waited. They hadn't reloaded the barrels, which clearly proved they had been in there only to hide the boat she'd stolen to escape with Telmund. Now there was plenty of room in the back for both prisoners.

"We going to tie him?" Jud asked.

"Nay," Willum said. "We're running short on rope. He won't be coming round proper till tomorrow. 'Twixt now and then, he won't know his hand from his foot. And meanwhile, that'll be long after we deliver both of 'em to the prince."

Wherever HE is, Amelia thought. By now, Prince Sheridan must surely have noticed she was missing, but there was no knowing if he had stayed at the hunting lodge to coordinate pursuit, or if he was tracking them, or if he was even now heading back to his castle to prepare for his upcoming marriage ceremony. *Their* upcoming marriage ceremony. Had the prince found some official of the church who would actually perform the rite—even if he saw Amelia was unwilling?

The two men propped her up, sitting with her back to the front wall of the cart. Telmund was tossed coldly onto the floor of the wagon beside her.

Once the men got the gray horse moving, Amelia nudged Telmund with her foot.

While *she* had been under the effects of the henbane, she had revived multiple times. Befuddled and sleepy, but awake.

What would that mean for Telmund and his uncommon-even-for-someone-familiar-with-stories spell?

She nudged him harder, guessing that he was probably having dreams as confused and disturbing as those she'd suffered through. "Wake up," she whispered. "Wake up, wake up."

Uncooperatively, he did not.

The four of them would make much better time than she and Telmund had on their own. For one thing, as morning progressed, there was more light to see by. In addition, since Willum and Jud weren't afraid of pursuit, they could follow the path without concern for moving quietly. And of course even the tired gray horse pulling the cart could make better time than a person walking.

But even given all that, they had been traveling for hardly any time at all when Jud pulled up on the reins to stop the horse.

They could *not* have made it back to the hunting lodge, Amelia thought, turning to look in the direction they were traveling.

Worse.

If Willum and Jud had returned her to the lodge, there would have been the chance that Prince Sheridan might have left, and that would have delayed another encounter with him. Anything could happen in the time it would take to get her to him.

Instead, Prince Sheridan had found *them*.

He and a good two dozen of his friends from the hunting lodge.

"Where have *you* been?" he demanded sourly of his two appointed kidnappers. "And I don't want to hear any feeble excuses." But in another moment his gaze slipped beyond the two men in the front of the cart to her in the back. "You!" he exclaimed before anybody had a chance to make excuses of any sort.

He dismounted and strode toward where she sat. "You are starting to become more troublesome than you are worth!" he bellowed.

For the second time in as many days, he grabbed hold of her by the hair, and this time it could only be called roughly—so roughly that Amelia suspected he planned to hoist her up out of the cart.

"And who is this?" Prince Sheridan demanded, catching sight of the sleeping Telmund. He used his free hand—his free fist— to jab into Telmund's side.

Telmund rolled over. One eye fluttered. Then opened. The eye grew suddenly huge, amber-colored, and slit-pupiled like a cat's. A moment later, his body expanded all in one instant into a massive flurry of talons, wings, and scales too big for the cart to hold. The boards forming the sides and bed of the cart cracked, and at the same time the wheels buckled under the weight, stranding the cart dead in its tracks.

Amelia would have screamed for added dramatic effect, but she couldn't coordinate her brain (intent), her muscles (open her mouth), and her vocal cords (sound).

No matter. The dragon emerging from Telmund's shape got everyone's attention.

He was easily the size of a small barn. He flicked his tail like an annoyed cat, never seeming to notice that he took down two elms and a willow in the process. His bronze-colored scales were sharp, his talons were sharp, his teeth were sharp. And speaking of teeth, he had an incredible number of them. Amelia, who was making herself as small as possible in the one surviving corner of the cart, got a too-close view of them as the dragon opened his mouth. It looked as though he planned to take a big chomp out of the surrounding forest.

Instead, with a ferocious roar, the dragon sent a blast of sulfur-tanged flame over Prince Sheridan's head.

The two erstwhile kidnappers dove off the seat. They abandoned cart, horse, prisoners, and each other, running in opposite directions into the woods.

157

The dragon sent crackling tongues of flame after each of them, but he didn't have enough control of his aim to actually hit either one.

Or maybe he had exactly the amount of control he wanted.

Slowly, the dragon turned his colossal head to face Prince Sheridan.

Using the grip he still had on her hair, Prince Sheridan yanked Amelia up onto her feet and hauled her out from the ruins of the cart. He spun her around so that she faced the dragon. He was using her as a shield.

"I offer you this maiden," Prince Sheridan told the dragon. "She's a princess, and you can feast on her flesh and bones."

"What?" Amelia demanded. "I thought I was to be your bride."

"At the moment, this is a more prudent political decision."

The dragon's head wavered from side to side.

Trying to find a way to get to Prince Sheridan without harming her? (That would have been Amelia's first-choice explanation of the movement.)

Trying to distract its victim like a snake? (Nothing wrong with that explanation, either—so long as the dragon maintained enough of Telmund's mind to recognize her, making the intended victim Prince Sheridan.)

Trying to stay awake as the henbane began to shut down his brain? (Very, very bad explanation.)

Prince Sheridan took a step backward, dragging Amelia with him.

"Or," he offered, "take my men standing here before you. I won't resist you."

The men shouldn't have been startled, knowing him as they did, but Amelia could see they were.

Prince Sheridan said, "Spare me, and I will make arrangements for you to be given all you want. All the gold, all the maidens, all the children. It doesn't make any difference to me."

The dragon was beginning to lower his head. His eyes were beginning to narrow.

No! No! No! Amelia thought.

But anyone not knowing about the henbane would have taken his movements as ferocity, as focusing, as intent to move.

Prince Sheridan shoved Amelia at the dragon. She stumbled to her knees, sliding forward on the ground, her outstretched and still-bound hands making contact with dragon scales, but luckily only on the smooth surface, not the jagged edge.

The dragon lowered his head even more. Toward her.

Amelia looked over her shoulder in time to see Prince Sheridan dart off into the trees.

A moment later, the other men scattered, leaving her to her fate.

"Coward!" she yelled after Prince Sheridan. "Your people would be wise to rebel against someone so eager to offer them and their families up in your stead!"

The horse didn't have the option to flee, fastened as it was to the ruins of the cart on which the dragon still sat. The horse tugged futilely, then lay down on the road, perhaps preparing to die.

"Good job, Telmund," Amelia said, trusting what he had told her about sharing his brain with whatever animal he'd turned

159

into. Of course, the henbane madness might be confusing things. Not that she could have run away, in any case, with her hands tied. "Good job. You've scared them away. Now we can head off home."

The dragon looked at her with unblinking eyes.

"It's me, Telmund," she said. "It's Amelia. You've been working very hard to rescue me, and now you have. You truly are a hero, and now we can go home."

The dragon looked up into the sky. Either his eyes were much better than hers or he wasn't really looking at anything. Nothing that was there, anyway.

"Good job, Telmund," Amelia repeated. It couldn't hurt to keep using his name, to remind him who he was. "Thank you for rescuing me, Telmund. Let's go home now."

The dragon sighed, emitting smoke only, no flame, and settled down into the splintered wood that had formerly been the cart.

"Or sleep," Amelia said. "That's good, too. But before you fall asleep . . ." She held her bound wrists out to him, thinking his multitude of very sharp teeth would make short work of the rope.

But it was already too late.

"Telmund," Amelia called. "Telmund."

Would the men come back? Amelia doubted it, not with a dragon having chased them away.

In any case, she was fairly confident Prince Sheridan would not. And certainly his men had seen they had no reason to be loyal to him.

But she also knew people did not always act the way you might expect them to.

"Telmund," she urged.

His body deflated, shrinking and twisting. The scales lost their luster and melted into one another, until they weren't scales at all anymore but had transformed into skin and clothing.

He turned back into a boy but never was fully awake enough to respond.

"Telmund. Telmund. Telmund."

His shape changed again—the process made her slightly queasy, but she couldn't look away—with some parts thickening and others thinning, and fur sprouting everywhere. He woke up briefly as a goat, just long enough to eat through her bindings.

She left the goat sleeping and released the horse from what was left of the cart.

The horse seemed to have gotten over having been so close to a dragon. It stood calmly, while Amelia did the best she could with shortening its reins. She had never ridden bareback before—if you didn't count being scrunched in front of Prince Sheridan's saddle, which she certainly didn't *want* to count. But even with just about no bareback experience, she knew she should not stay here, nor could she travel by foot with Telmund, whose senses wouldn't return till tomorrow.

She went back to where she'd left the goat and found a snake. Well, a snake would be easier to pick up than a goat—or a boy, for that matter. As uneasy as the thought of picking up a snake made her, she told herself she was fortunate she'd missed a couple transformations.

Amelia had to tell herself this a total of four times before she could actually pick up the snake.

"Everything is fine, Telmund," she assured him.

Luckily, he wasn't a very long snake. She draped him over the neck of the horse (the horse was not overjoyed, either), and then Amelia scrambled up behind him. "Adders are not aggressive," she told the horse, told herself. "And, even if they *do* bite, their bite isn't usually fatal." She repeated *this*, too, for good measure. "Not usually."

Then, with one hand on the snake so he wouldn't slide off, she got the horse moving in the direction toward Pastonia. She could tell exactly where they were by the shape of the mountains in the distance and the knowledge that the river was to her right.

Telmund woke up midmorning as himself and spent a little time sitting up with Amelia on the horse's back, her arms holding him steady as he babbled about the fact that he would *not* be good to eat.

"Definitely not," Amelia reassured him. "I know. You're safe with me."

Her voice seemed to soothe him.

"Tell me a story," he mumbled.

"Oh," she had to admit, "I don't know any."

His voice a hoarse whisper, Telmund said, "Tell me one anyway."

She couldn't very well tell the little bit of the story that she'd remembered earlier, in the straw wagon, the story that her father had upset her with when she'd been a small child: *Once*

162

upon a time, there was a little pig who built his house of straw. Because straw is a very inadequate building material, a wolf came along and ate him up, but apparently another pig survived.

To keep him calm, and to help pass the time, and because she suspected he wouldn't remember a word of what she said, Amelia started telling the only story she knew: her own. "Once upon a time," she told him, because as little as she knew about stories, she knew that's the way they start, "there was a princess whose parents were perfectly lovely people. But this was a problem, because their total loveliness made them unrealistic in their outlooks. They assumed everybody else was perfectly lovely, too, and that, therefore, nothing truly bad could ever happen. Yes, there would be minor setbacks and inconveniences, but a pleasant disposition and a sunny outlook could help fix just about every problem, and eventually all lives would always reach the stage of 'And they lived happily ever after.'"

She thought once again about that one story and amended: "Except, maybe, for certain pigs. Anyway, their daughter, the princess, recognized that her parents loved her, just as she loved them, no matter how different she was from them. But she didn't feel she was as safe as they kept telling her she was. She felt that if she understood the world, she would be better prepared. Prepared to protect herself and her kingdom and even her parents. And so she devoted herself to the gathering of facts."

Amelia stopped talking. She didn't know where the story would go from there.

Either Telmund was very patient or he hadn't been listening. He didn't urge her to continue.

In fact, he was growing more and more droopy. At the same time, the landscape was growing more and more familiar.

Amelia kept a careful watch on him as he slept and saw the moment he twitched once, then began to shrink.

The next moment, she was holding a hedgehog.

Her fingers, already sore from holding on so tightly to the reins, keenly felt the prickles of his spines. But she was more than willing to forgive him, for his newly wiggly nose was absolutely adorable.

She fashioned a sling by ripping material from the bottom of her dress, and that was how she and Telmund arrived at the castle.

"Your Highness!" The men from the guard stationed at the gate shouted at her in a tone she interpreted to mean that they had never thought to see her again.

Just as noticeably, they had never thought to see her astride a horse, and bearing a sleeping hedgehog.

Amelia dismounted and handed the horse's reins to one of the guards. But she didn't hand over the hedgehog.

"Send word to my parents that I will join them as soon as I can. But there is one thing I must do first." She knew her parents would be sick with worry, and she had never been more eager for anything than she was to see them, to hug them, to tell them all that had happened, and to be comforted by them.

But she owed Telmund a debt that *must* be repaid.

She'd thought about his fairy in the garden for much of the while she had ridden, and she realized how unmindful she must have been the night of the ball. So now, instead of entering the castle, she returned to the bench where she'd been sitting when she'd met the strange ageless girl.

"Animal in trouble!" Amelia called out. "Hedgehog in dire danger!" The men accompanying her looked at one another fretfully, obviously concerned for her wits. "Fairy needed!" Amelia called. "Where are you? This hedgehog needs assistance!"

"The hedgehog is fine," a quiet voice said from behind her—which meant Amelia had walked right by her without noticing. "There's nothing I can do for him."

The guards were clearly taken by surprise to find a stranger this close to their just-recovered princess. They went to draw their swords, but Amelia held her hand out to forestall them.

How could she not have noticed the wings, even given that the night had been dark? And the hair wasn't light blonde bleached by the moonlight: It was unmistakably silver.

"He's not supposed to *be* a hedgehog," Amelia said. "There's nothing at all *fine* about his situation."

"Not my spell," the fairy told her. "Nothing I can do about it."

"But he's in danger," Amelia said, "because he's *supposed* to be human."

"But he's *not* in danger as a hedgehog," the fairy insisted. "Not unless you drop him."

"I will," Amelia threatened. "I'll *throw* him." He was sound asleep, curled up into a tight, if prickly, ball.

The fairy gave a knowing smile. "No, you won't," she said with total confidence.

Amelia held the hedgehog in her hand. She couldn't bring herself to do it, for what if the fairy still didn't intervene? It was Telmund's best chance, but it was too big a risk. "You're not exactly tenderhearted, are you?" Amelia pointed out.

The fairy shrugged. "I did give your wish a nudge," she said.

"My—?" Amelia remembered meeting the fairy girl the night of the ball. They had talked about wishes. And Amelia had said that—if she believed in wishes—what she'd wish for was a solution to the problem of Prince Sheridan. She said, "If that *was* you, that was a rather inefficient, thoroughly distressing, and potentially disastrous way of causing my wish to come true."

The fairy shrugged again. "It was a nudge."

Was it anything to do with her? Amelia wondered.

But just then she heard her mother cry out her name. She looked up and saw both her parents were running toward her. A moment later, when she tried to find the fairy again, she was gone.

And then Amelia was enveloped in her parents' arms.

Chapter 12

Ending

TELMUND

Telmund opened his eyes. He waited to get hit by the muzzy, head-stuffed-with-something-that-was-simultaneously-jagged-and-squishy-and-whatever-else-it-was-*definitely*-unpleasant sensation that came from whatever Willum had dosed him with. But that didn't happen.

He let his eyes focus.

He was in his own room. His mother was sitting across from him, working on a piece of embroidery. Though he hadn't made a noise, she chose that very moment to look up at him—or maybe she was constantly looking up to check on him. That is, after all, what mothers do.

A thirteen-year-old youth, even one who wasn't *trying* to be the hero of his own life story, shouldn't be so relieved to see his mother, he told himself as his eyes filled with tears that then began running down his cheeks.

It's probably not even really her, he told himself next. In another moment she would burst into being a singing geranium—this had actually happened one of the previous times he'd thought his head was clear.

But it hadn't felt *this* clear, and in the next instant his mother set down the cloth she was stitching, stood, and placed a cool hand on his forehead.

"Are you back, Little One?" It was the name she'd had for him before Wilmar had been born. It was silly to be jealous of his younger brother over this, but that was just the way things were.

She used the end of her sleeve to mop up his tear-and-snot-dampened face. "There, there," she cooed. "You're back. You're safe. It's all over."

Much as he wanted to keep hearing her murmur reassurances, Telmund shook his head. "I'm not. It's not. I have a spell on me. Unless we can somehow find—"

"Shhh," she hushed him. "We know all about that. We've been hearing all about how brave and resourceful and persevering you've been. Your father and I—the whole family—we're all so proud of you."

Telmund didn't think he'd ever been told this before. Maybe his *mother* had been proud of him for little childish accomplishments, but not his father. Not his brothers.

And there was no reason for them to be proud of him now.

He didn't know what they'd heard, but once he explained what had really happened and how he'd muddled through everything, they'd all say, "Oh. Well. That sounds more like the Telmund we know."

168

Princess Amelia must have escaped capture and gotten help after he'd allowed himself to be ambushed by Prince Sheridan's men. Then she'd arranged for him to be brought home. It was embarrassing to think he needed to be rescued by the princess he'd hoped to rescue. And it even sounded as though she'd done her best to hide how not-up-to the adventure he'd been.

But that wasn't the worst thing. The worst thing was that—even if the nightmares about singing geraniums (not to mention the tiara-wearing hens who'd kept asking him, "Who do you think you are?")—even if that part of the ordeal was over, as soon as he fell asleep, he'd wake up as yet another creature.

Words failed him, and Telmund shook his head.

His mother turned away from him, no doubt dismayed by his self-pity.

But it turned out she was simply gesturing for someone behind her to approach.

Wilmar came up beside Telmund's bed. "Hello, Telmund," his little brother said softly, as though afraid sheer volume of voice might cause Telmund to break.

Set a good example, Telmund told himself. *Stop sniveling.*

Before he had a chance to act on this, he realized that Wilmar wasn't alone—someone was coming up behind him.

Telmund hoped he hadn't been making such an unseemly show of himself in front of his father, or one of his brothers, or even Princess Amelia—not that she had any reason to be here.

Which was sad. He hadn't even had a chance to say good-bye. He wouldn't have told her this, but he had actually begun to . . . get used to her.

All right, all right: to admire her.

Maybe even (he was never going to see her again, so he could admit it to himself) . . . to like her.

But it wasn't father, brother, or princess who came up behind Wilmar, resting hands on the boy's shoulders and giving Telmund a not-one-whit-apologetic smile. It was the old witch from the festival grounds.

If Telmund had been able to burrow backward through his mattress, he would have.

Let this be another of my crazy-headed visions, he prayed, *along with the jousting worms riding on the backs of ladybird beetles.*

"Now, now," the old witch said, showing her crooked gray teeth. "Don't be alarmed."

Wilmar proudly announced, "Look, Telmund! We didn't have to find *her.* She found *us.*"

The old witch nodded.

If that was meant to reassure him, it did the opposite.

"Don't be cranky, now," the old witch said. "I'm not the one who threw you into the river."

"I told them that," Wilmar said. "I told everybody everything." He leaned forward to add in an impressed whisper, "The steward has been put on rat-grooming duty for what he did."

That was so unexpected and perplexing, Telmund was jolted a little bit out of his oh-no-what's-she-going-to-do-to-me-now anxiety. He asked, "He's on what?"

"Rat-grooming duty," Wilmar repeated. "He has to capture all the rats he can, and he has to do it without harming them. And he has to bathe them and brush them and feed them and house them in nice clean cages and keep them company and talk agreeably to them. Father decreed it while you were missing, because we didn't know how far away you'd gone, so any one of the rats could have been you. Once you came back, the steward asked if he could stop now, but Father says he must continue for ten times as long as you were gone." Wilmar looked over to where their mother was standing and added, "And Mother told him he must sing lullabies to the rats every night."

Their mother waved her hand airily, as though none of that was important. "Mistress Elmina came forward when we were looking for you."

"I kept hearing all these nice things about you," the old witch said. (Telmund could not think of her as anything *but* the old witch.) "It's not uncommon for parents to be hoodwinked by their thoroughly wicked children, but people in the town were singing your praises, too."

Singing geraniums, Telmund thought, because his thinking wasn't quite as clear as it could have been.

The witch said, "And I thought to myself: *What if I've been unduly hasty?* So I went back to that merchant who was selling wooden bowls. He was hiding in the corner of his booth with a blanket over his head after hearing that I was looking for him. But once I ferreted him out, he told me what he had seen that day. Then I sought out young Wilmar here. He told me much the same story. *Everybody* tells me you're not a bad boy; you're not a bully. Maybe not the born leader people might expect a prince should be, nor the bravest, nor the smartest, nor—"

Telmund's mother cleared her throat.

"All right, all right," the witch said. "So I went to your parents, and I explained that I could still feel the spell out in the world, so you had *not* drowned in the river, and all these older brothers of yours came to town along with their assorted wives and children and fellow monks, and they all joined in scouring the banks of the river searching for you, until someone found you in Pastonia. Seems the princess there had brought you back to her parents' home. You were a swan by the time you got back here."

"Of course I was," Telmund said wearily.

The old witch finished by saying, "So, Telmund, if you can prove to me you're not a bully, the spell will go away."

Prove? Telmund thought. *How am I supposed to do that?*

Wilmar said to the witch, "But I already *told* you."

"Yes," she said. "And there could be many reasons you might *tell* me something untrue."

Wilmar began to cry. "I'm sorry, Telmund. I didn't *mean* for this to happen to you. I'm sorry, I'm sorry, I'm sorry."

Their mother made a move as though to sweep in to comfort Wilmar, but Telmund got to him first by draping him with an arm and enclosing him in a protective embrace. "Stop it," he said. If he couldn't be a hero, at least he could stop his little brother from feeling bad. "You didn't do anything wrong. I'm the one who's sorry. I may not bully you, but I'm not always the older brother I should be. I'm sorry for those times I get impatient with you. I'm sorry for those times I forget that you aren't

172

me, and so I get annoyed when you say or do things differently from how I would. I'm sorry I'm not the best older brother to you that I could be."

"But you are!" Wilmar said, throwing his arms around Telmund's neck and hugging him.

Telmund didn't even cringe that his little brother's hands were sticky from something-or-other.

He did, however, cringe when a strange sensation washed over him. It felt as though his skin was bubbling and rippling, too big and saggy over his bones. He looked down at his arm around Wilmar, and waited to see if it would sprout fur, feathers, or scales.

His skin—which fit exactly right over his bones—didn't change at all.

The old witch showed her gray teeth again. "Done!" she said. "See, that wasn't so hard, was it?" Then she added, "And now, as much fun as this has been, just in case your father won't let bygones be bygones, as he indicated should I remove the spell . . ." And she made spirally gestures with the pointer fingers of both hands and disappeared.

AMELIA

Amelia and her parents were strolling through the Rosenmark gardens, guests of the royal family, when King Leopold sent word that his second-youngest son was recovered, both from the effects of the henbane and from the transforming spell.

"You may visit him now, if you wish," invited the servant King Leopold had sent, a rather short man who looked tired, spoke hoarsely, and for some reason had a rat riding on his shoulder.

Amelia and her parents didn't comment on the rat and followed the servant back into the castle.

"I'm most eager to meet this young man of yours," her father told Amelia.

Amelia felt her face go red. "He's not my young man," she said in a lowered voice so the servant wouldn't overhear.

"He's *a* young man," her father said, not catching the hint, so not lowering his voice at all.

"About whom you've been very worried," her mother added, just as unmindful as Amelia's father.

Amelia said, "Well, yes. I'm grateful to him for having rescued me." It was certainly all right for the servant to hear that.

"As I'm sure he is grateful to you for having rescued him," her father said.

"Maybe not quite so much as the other way around," her mother observed. "Male pride being what it is."

"But, still, in the end . . ." her father said.

"In the end," her mother agreed. "The two of you made a very good partnership, and that's important."

"Partnership?" Amelia echoed. She had her suspicions where this conversation was headed. Her voice got louder, all by itself. "He's thirteen. I'm fifteen." It was one thing to like the boy; it was pushy of her parents to make presumptions.

Her father laughed. "Someday that won't seem such a big difference."

The servant stopped and held the door open, letting the three of them into Telmund's room. Then he and his rat left.

Telmund looked as startled as though someone had just dumped a bucket of cold water on him. By the way he sat up in bed and adjusted the blanket and ran his fingers through his hair, Amelia suspected no one had warned him they were coming. He looked as young as ever, but he also looked happy to see her. And—she could admit it to herself, if not to her parents—she was also happy to see him.

She said, "Father, Mother, may I present Prince Telmund of Rosenmark."

Her father shook Telmund's hand. "Thank you, young man, for rescuing our daughter from Prince Sheridan."

"The odious Prince Sheridan," her mother added.

Telmund blushed. "But I didn't," he said. "I only *tried*."

"Nonsense," Amelia said. "You rescued me repeatedly." In the spirit of total frankness, she had to add, "True, I rescued you once or twice also, but that doesn't diminish what *you* did. And you turned into a *dragon*. It's not every story hero who gets to do that."

"I don't remember it," Telmund admitted. "My mother said you told her that happened, but . . ." He shook his head.

"Prince Sheridan remembers," Amelia said, "that's the important thing. And his people who were there with him. They saw him cowering and afraid. They heard him offering them and their loved ones up in his place. They were ready to rise up in rebellion."

Her father finished, "The only thing that prevented that was when old King Whitcomb signed a proclamation naming one of his nephews as heir to the throne in Sheridan's place."

Astonished, Telmund asked, "And Prince Sheridan agreed to that?"

"He didn't get a chance to," Amelia said. "While I was his prisoner, he'd let it slip to me that he'd been betrothed before. Once I was home, I asked the fairy in our garden if she knew anything about that."

"Fairies are uncooperative," her father said. "But notorious busybodies."

"We only say that in the kindest, most grateful way," her mother amended, because she was always excruciatingly polite.

Amelia continued, "It turns out, the princess to whom Prince Sheridan was betrothed was the troll king's daughter. It also turns out that Prince Sheridan had lied to her: He'd sent word that he couldn't marry her, claiming he had entered the priesthood. I talked to the fairy in our garden, the fairy in our garden talked to the Fairy Council, the Fairy Council talked to the Troll Council, the Troll Council talked to the troll king, and the troll king came himself and fetched Prince Sheridan away to fulfill his obligations."

Her father said, "And as trolls are as arrogant and argumentative and unpleasant as he is, I'm sure it will be a fine match."

Her mother finished by announcing, "And to think I never knew we had a fairy in our garden!"

"Wow," Telmund said. "It sounds as though she was much more accommodating for you than she was for me."

"Well, she does live in our garden," Amelia pointed out to him, "so a certain amount of reciprocation might be expected. Still, the point is that none of this would have happened if you hadn't stepped in and rescued me. Repeatedly. It was very heroic. Just like in a story. Thank you."

For once he didn't argue. He smiled, inclined his head, and said, "You're welcome. I'm glad you don't have to worry about Prince Sheridan anymore. That must be a great relief."

It was Amelia's turn to nod. "And we have been given to understand that the witch who put the spell on you has taken it away?"

"Yes," Telmund said.

"That must be a great relief to you, also."

"Yes," Telmund said to that, too.

My goodness! thought Amelia. *How formal we're all being!*

She smiled at him, and he smiled back—but nervously. *He's unsure of himself,* she realized. He was probably unsure of her as well.

Despite all her facts, despite all his stories, neither of them felt secure about what to do.

She asked herself, *What would the hero of one of Telmund's stories do?*

Well, she decided—based on the stories she had been reading, one after the other, ever since she had gotten home—a hero would never be too afraid to act.

This thought gave her the courage to say, "All in all, I think we probably should have tried *this* to break your spell." And with that, Amelia leaned forward and kissed him.

And he kissed her.

And her parents, who believed in love at first sight and in happily ever after, kissed each other.

❧ *Beginning* ❧

That's much nicer than kissing a hen would have been, Telmund thought.

We're young, Amelia thought, *and things might change.*

Or they might not. In any case, it was a beginning. Maybe even a once-upon-a-time beginning.

About the Author

Vivian Vande Velde is the author of *The Princess Imposter* and the Edgar Award–winning *Never Trust a Dead Man*. She has also written *Heir Apparent*, *Dragon's Bait*, and dozens of other fantasy and mystery novels for young readers. She lives in Rochester, New York, with her husband, Jim.